BEN
A SK OF
HOPE

By

Ana Monroy

Copyright © 2025 by Ana Monroy

All rights reserved. No part of this book may be used or reproduced in any form whatsoever without written permission except in the case of brief quotations in critical articles or reviews.

This book is a work of fiction. Names, characters, businesses, organizations, places, events and incidents either are the product of the author's imagination or are used fictitiously. Any resemblance to actual persons, living or dead, events, or locales is entirely coincidental.

Printed in the United Kingdom.

For more information, or to book an event, contact:
Email: ana.monroy@rocketmail.com
Website: https://www.amazon.co.uk

Book design by Kindlepreneur
Cover design by Book Cover Generator

ISBN - Paperback: 9798288599378

First Edition: June 2025

"When one is in love, one always begins by deceiving oneself, and one always ends by deceiving others. That is what the world calls a romance,"

"I think the best thing you can do is just love someone and take a chance,"

Agatha Christie

Beneath a Sky of Hope

Ana Monroy

CONTENTS

Acknowledgements

Chapter 1: The Crash Landing

Chapter 2: The Hidden Refuge

Chapter 3: Crossing Paths

Chapter 4: A Dangerous Alliance

Chapter 5: The Enemy's Grip

Chapter 6: A Fragile Connection

Chapter 7: Tempests of War

Chapter 8: Shelter in the Storm

Chapter 9: Unlikely Companions

Chapter 10: The Bond Deepens

Chapter 11: Echoes of Conflict

Chapter 12: The War Within

Chapter 13: A Dangerous Mission

Chapter 14: The Tides of Change

Chapter 15: Shadows at the Edge

Chapter 16: The Sound of Something New

Chapter 17: A Quiet Proposal

Chapter 18: A Thread Across the Sea

Chapter 19: When The Light Finds Her

Authors Note

Acknowledgements

This book is dedicated to my father John Monroy and late mother Jane Sylvester who have been my inspiration throughout my life on and off, they have always believed in me to always follow my dreams.

1

Beneath a Sky of Hope

The Crash Landing

The roar of the engine thrums through my body, a familiar rhythm that has become as essential as the very air I breathe. Up here, high above the lush landscapes of Sicily, I feel a sense of freedom, a fleeting moment when the chaos of the world below seems far away. But that freedom is short-lived. The radio crackles with urgent orders, and the adrenaline surges as I bank the plane, ready to engage in another dogfight. Suddenly, a sharp jolt rattles me. I grip the controls tighter as the plane shudders, a violent tremor that sends my heart racing. The warning lights flicker on the dashboard, a cacophony of alarms screaming for my attention. I glance at the gauges; the fuel is dangerously low. Panic rises in my throat like bile. I can't let it end like this—not here, not now. I wrestle with the controls, my instincts kicking in.

The horizon tilts as I struggle to correct the descent, the landscape below a blur of green and brown. The war-torn beauty of Sicily stretches out beneath me, the hills rolling like waves, dotted with patches of olive groves and the occasional cluster of white-washed villas. I can almost picture the villagers going about their lives, unaware of the turmoil above. But that vision shatters as the plane begins to plummet, the earth rushing up to meet me. The engine sputters, a dying gasp that sends a cold shiver down my spine. I fight against it, but the plane has other plans. With a final, gut-wrenching lurch, I pull the stick back as hard as I can, attempting to level out. The world tilts violently, and I brace for impact, my heart pounding in my chest. I close my eyes for a fleeting moment, as if that could shield me from the impending crash.

A bone-jarring thud reverberates through the fuselage, followed by a sickening crunch. The plane skids across the rough terrain, metal screeching against the earth, the stench of burning fuel filling the cockpit. I'm thrown violently against the harness, the world outside spinning into chaos. Dust and debris whirl around me, the cacophony of destruction drowning out my thoughts.

When in my world finally still, I sit there, disoriented, heart racing, and take a moment to breathe deeply, inhaling the acrid smoke that fills the cabin. I shake my head to clear the fog, my senses reeling as I assess the damage. The cockpit is a wreck, smoke curling from the engine, and the sound of distant explosions rumbles in the air like a sinister lullaby. I unbuckle the harness, my fingers trembling as the weight of the situation crashes down on me. I force the door open, wincing at the screech of metal that feels like it echoes through my very bones. The sunlight spills in, illuminating the wreckage and the surrounding landscape. I step out gingerly, my boots crunching against shards of twisted metal and dirt. The air is thick with tension, the distant sounds of war a constant reminder of the danger lurking beyond my immediate surroundings.

I take a moment, scanning the horizon. The hills rise majestically around me, their craggy outlines softened by the vibrant greens and browns of summer. But beneath that beauty lies an undercurrent of fear. I have no idea how far behind enemy lines I've landed, and I can feel the urgency creeping in—the relentless tick of time reminding me that I need to move. My first instinct is to search for shelter, a place to hide from the German forces that could be scouring the area. The village I spotted in the air is nearby; I have no idea what kind of reception I'll receive there. I'm a British fighter pilot, an enemy in their midst. I swallow hard, forcing my legs to move as I pick a path through the rubble of my once-mighty aircraft. As I make my way down the hillside, the warm sun beats down on my back, a stark contrast to the chill of fear coiling in my gut. The beauty of the landscape is overwhelming, wildflowers bloom in vibrant patches, and the scent of sunbaked earth fills the air. But I can't afford to admire the scenery. I must keep moving. The village draws closer, and I can hear the faint sounds of life—a child's laughter, the distant murmur of voices, the clattering of pots. My heart races at the thought of people, of potential allies, but the fear of being discovered grips me tightly.

I slip into the shadows, the craggy hills offering some semblance of cover as I navigate toward the heart of the village. Just as I reach the outskirts, I spot a group of children playing a game, their laughter is ringing like bells in the afternoon sun. They are so innocent, so untouched by the horrors of war. For a moment, I feel a pang of longing for normalcy, for the days before the war which had intruded upon everything. But that longing is quickly overshadowed by the reality of my situation. I cannot reveal myself; I cannot undermine their safety. I retreated further into the shadows, my breath quickening. The village may be my only chance for survival; the risks are immense. I watch the children from a distance, their carefree movements a stark contrast to the turmoil within me. I need to find a way to reach out, to communicate, I know my presence could spell disaster. As the sun begins to dip toward the horizon, painting the sky in hues of orange and pink, I feel a flicker of hope.

If I can just find one person willing to help, someone who understands the stakes, perhaps I can survive this nightmare. But first, I must tread carefully, for beneath the Sicilian sky, danger lurks in every shadow. The sun hangs high in the Sicilian sky, casting a golden hue over the rugged landscape. I can still feel the remnants of adrenaline coursing through my veins, a stark contrast to the tranquil beauty surrounding me. My heart races as I step out of the wreckage, the twisted metal of my fighter plane, a grim reminder of how suddenly everything can change. The engine's fire sputters into silence, leaving behind the faint acrid smell of burning fuel, mingling with the earthy aroma of the Mediterranean. I scan my surroundings; my senses are heightened. The deep green hills roll gently into the distance, dotted with clusters of wildflowers swaying in the warm breeze.

This beauty is a fleeting moment in times like these, and I force myself to focus on the immediate danger: I am stranded in enemy territory, with no idea how far I am from safety. The distant rumble of artillery reminds me that war is not just a backdrop; it is all consuming, a monster lurking just beyond the horizon. I take a cautious step away from the wreckage, my boots crunching on the gravel beneath me. The village I can barely see in the distance seems

untouched—an oasis of normalcy amidst the chaos. I need to get there, but I can't risk being spotted. The German forces have a tight grip on Sicily, and my uniform makes me a prime target. I pull my jacket tighter around me, trying to blend into the scenery like a shadow. As I start to move, fear gnaws at my insides. I've trained for aerial combat, not this, being on the ground, exposed and vulnerable. Each step feels like a leap into the unknown. I remember the faces of my squadron, the camaraderie we forged in the sky, and I long for that safety. But
I can't dwell on what I've lost; I must press forward.

The path leads me through a cluster of olive trees, their gnarled branches twisting against the blue sky like ancient hands reaching for something lost. I pause to catch my breath, leaning against a sturdy trunk. The leaves rustle softly, almost as if trying to soothe my anxiety. I close my eyes for a moment, allowing the peaceful sounds of nature to wash over me, but the urgency of my situation quickly pulls me back to reality. I take one last look at the wreckage, a dark silhouette against the vibrant landscape, before turning toward the village. My heart pounds as I move forward, each step a reminder that I'm a lone soldier in a vast world at war. As I approach the outskirts, the sounds of life begin to filter through, the laughter of children, the soft murmur of elders, the clinking of the pots and pans.

It is surreal, almost dissonant against the backdrop of conflict. I glimpse a few villagers tending to their daily routines, blissfully unaware of the chaos that looms just beyond their borders. I duck behind a wall, my mind racing with possibilities. What if they see me? What if they mistake me for a German soldier? I take a deep breath, trying to quell the rising panic. I can't afford to be reckless. I need to find a way to communicate, to seek help without inciting fear. Suddenly, I spot a woman emerge from a small stone cottage, her silhouette framed by the doorway. She carries a basket filled with fresh bread, the warm scent wafting toward me, tantalizing and grounding. I watch her for a moment, captivated by the way she moves with purpose, her long dark hair cascading down her back, catching the sunlight.

There's an undeniable strength in her stance, a quiet resolve that draws me in. But I can't linger. The village is alive, and I need to remain hidden. I slip past the cottage, heart racing as I navigate the narrow alleyways, careful to stay out of sight. I can hear snippets of conversation, laughter, and the occasional shouts, but I remain focused on my goal: to find refuge and figure out my next move.

As I round a corner, I enter a small square bustling with activity. Villagers gather around a well, exchanging news and gossip. I spot an old man gesturing animatedly, while a group of children play nearby, their laughter ringing like music in the air. It's a stark contrast to the chaos I've just escaped, and for a moment, I feel a pang of longing for the simplicity of life before the war. But I'm still a target. I need to keep moving.

I eventually find a nook between two buildings where I can observe without being seen. The woman from earlier enters the square, her basket is now empty. She pauses with her eyes scanning the area, and for a moment, our gazes lock. There's a flicker of recognition, a shared understanding that transcends language. She seems to sense the urgency in my presence, though she cannot know my story. As the villagers disperse, I take a chance and step out from my hiding place. My heart pounds in my chest as I approach her, aware that I'm crossing an invisible line between her world and mine. She watches me with a mix of curiosity and caution, her brow furrowing slightly. I raise my hands, palms out, a gesture of peace. "Please," I say, my voice low yet steady. "I need help." Her eyes widen slightly, and I can see the conflict playing out on her face. There's fear but also a flicker of compassion. I can't afford to waste time. I gesture toward the hills, then to myself, trying to convey the urgency of my situation.

For a moment, it feels like the weight of the world hangs between us, suspended in the air. Then, slowly, she nods, the tension in her shoulders easing just a fraction. She glances around, ensuring no one else is watching, then gestures for me to follow her. I breathe a sigh of relief, the first glimmer of hope breaking through the clouds of uncertainty. Beneath the Sicilian sky, amidst the chaos of war, I've found an unexpected ally, a flicker of light in the dark. I follow her my heart racing not just from fear, but from the potential of what lies ahead.

I can see my plane burning and emitting black and grey smoke in the distance from the place I left behind. I gasp for breath, I am looking at another allied plane in the sky descending through the thick, humid air, the Sicilian landscape behind me is unfolding beneath me like a patchwork quilt of vibrant greens and browns. It's a chaotic mix of beauty and danger, and I feel it in my bones.

My heart is still pounding in my chest, the realization

slowly sinking in: I'm stranded in enemy territory. The villagers exchange glances, uncertainty etched across their faces. Just then, I feel a presence at my side. The same woman steps forward, with her dark hair cascading over her shoulders, her eyes is a deep shade of brown that seems to hold an entire world within them. There's an air of quiet strength about her. "Please," she says softly, her accent thick but her intent clear. "You shouldn't be here. It's not safe." "I crashed," I explain, gesturing towards the wreckage in the distance. "I need to find shelter, and I can help. I can fight." Her gaze searches for mine, and for a moment, I can see the struggle within her fear, concern, and something else, something that resonates deep within me. "We cannot take that risk," she finally replies, her voice firm yet gentle. "Then let me help you," I insist, desperation creeping into my tone. "I'm trained for this. I can help protect your village."

The villagers murmur among themselves, the tension in the air palpable. But the woman, the schoolteacher, I realize, holds her ground, studying me with a mix of determination and empathy. "What is your name?" she finally asks, her voice cutting through the noise. "Jack. Jack Branner." "Jack," she repeats, her expression softening slightly. "I am Elena Santoro." The name rolls off her tongue like music, and I find myself captivated. "Elena," I echo, the sound of it filling the space between us. She turns to the villagers, her voice rising above the din. "We must help him. He is not our enemy." A ripple of uncertainty passes through the group, but Elena's conviction is infectious. Slowly, their expressions shift from fear to reluctant acceptance. I feel a rush of gratitude, the first flicker of hope igniting in my chest.

"Come," she says, motioning for me to follow. "We have a hidden place where you can stay for now." As I walk beside her, I can't help but steal glances at her. There's a quiet strength in her, a resilience that draws me in. I know that beneath the chaos of war, there's something precious growing between me and her, a connection forged in the fires of desperation and hope.

I follow her deeper into the village, the sun dipping lowering in the sky, casting a warm glow over the cobblestones. In this moment, beneath the Sicilian sky, I feel a sense of purpose returning. I may be stranded, but I'm not alone. And with that realization, the glimmer of hope transforms into a burning flame, igniting my spirit as we step into the unknown together.

2

The Hidden Refuge

As the sun dips toward the horizon in Sicily, long shadows sweep over the rugged landscape. I sit quietly in a secluded corner of the cave, my heart still racing from the adrenaline of the crash. The air is thick with tension, a silent reminder of the chaos that rages beyond these stone walls. I can hear the distant rumble of artillery, the eerie wails of sirens echoing through the valley, but all of it fades into the background as my attention shifts to her. Elena is a vision, her dark hair cascading like a waterfall down her back, her eyes a deep, soulful brown that seem to absorb the world around her. She moves through the dim light of the cave with a grace that belies the uncertainty of our situation. Each step she takes is deliberate, purposeful, and I can't help but admire the strength that radiates from her. She's not just a young schoolteacher; she's a pillar of hope for the frightened villagers huddled in the shadows, seeking solace from the horrors outside.

I watch as she kneels beside a group of children, their faces pale with fear, eyes wide and glistening with unshed tears. She speaks softly to them, her voice a gentle balm to their frayed nerves. In that moment, I realize that her watchful eyes are not just observing the chaos; they are attuned to the needs of those around her. The way she comforts the children, brushing a stray tear from a little girl's cheek, makes my heart swell with something I can't quite define—admiration, perhaps, or something deeper?

Elena glances up and catches my gaze, her eyes piercing through the murkiness of my thoughts. There's an unspoken understanding between us, a connection that transcends language and circumstance. She doesn't seem afraid of me, despite the uniform I wear, the insignia that marks me as an enemy to many in this land. Instead, she regards me with a mixture of curiosity and compassion, as if she sees beyond the pilot and into the man who is desperately trying to find his place in this madness.

For a fleeting moment, I wonder what she sees when she looks at me. A soldier? A savior? Or perhaps just a lost soul searching for purpose? I want to ask her to delve deeper into her thoughts, but the fear of shattering this fragile moment holds me back. Instead, I simply return her gaze, hoping to convey the gratitude that wells up inside me. As the hours pass, Elena remains a steady presence amidst the turmoil. She organizes the villagers, assigning tasks to the older men, directing the women as they prepare meagre meals, all while keeping an eye on the children who dart around, trying to reclaim a sense of normalcy. The cave transforms under her guidance; it becomes a sanctuary, a refuge from the storm that brews outside. I can't help but admire the way she commands respect, how her quiet authority brings a sense of order to the chaos.

I find myself drawn to her, wanting to understand the depth of her resolve. She's a woman of strength, not just in her actions but in the way she carries herself, shoulders back, chin up, even when the world around her threatens to crumble. I can see the weariness etched into her features, the shadows beneath her eyes that tell tales of sleepless nights spent worrying for her village, for her students, for a future that feels increasingly uncertain. Yet, there's also a fire within her, a fierce determination that flickers brightly, illuminating the darkness.

One of the village elders approaches her, his face lined with age and wear. They exchange words in hushed tones, and I can see the worry etched on his brow. Elena listens intently, her expression shifting from concern to resolve. She nods, and I can see her mind racing, plotting a course of action that could keep them safe.

It's in these moments that I recognize the true weight of her burden. She's not just protecting her home; she's safeguarding the very essence of her community. As the day wears on, the rumble of distant gunfire becomes more pronounced, each sound a reminder of the reality we're all trying to escape. The children, once lively and vibrant, grow quiet as fear seeps back into the cave like a creeping shadow. Elena senses it, too; I can see the way her shoulders are tense, the way her hands clench into fists at her sides. She takes a deep breath, and I can almost see her gathering her strength, stealing herself for what comes next.

"Listen," she says, her voice rising above the murmurs of

uncertainty, "we are safe here for now. But we must be brave, for each other. Remember, fear is only as strong as we allow it to be." Her words resonate with the villagers, and as I watch them rally around her, I feel an unexpected swell of pride. This is her domain, and she is their protector, their beacon of hope in a world that seems intent on swallowing them whole.

But as I sit there, torn between my admiration for her resilience and the chaos that looms beyond the cave, I can't shake the feeling that our fates are irrevocably intertwined. She glances at me again, and this time, her expression shifts—there's an understanding in her eyes that speaks to the uncharted territory of our lives. I'm a soldier, and she's a teacher, yet here we are, bound together by circumstance, sharing a moment of fragile humanity. In the midst of war, beneath this Sicilian sky, I realize that it's not just survival we're fighting for; it's connection. It's the understanding that even in the darkest times, love can bloom in the most unexpected places. As the sun begins its descent, casting a warm golden hue over the cave, I find myself hoping—hoping that whatever tomorrow brings, we will face it together, under the watchful eyes of Elena Santoro.

Elena stands at the edge of the village, a fragile silhouette against the backdrop of the rugged Sicilian hills. The sun hangs low in the sky, casting a golden hue over the olive groves and craggy stone cottages, but her heart is heavy. As the echoes of distant artillery reverberate through the air, she knows that the peaceful image of her homeland is marred by the creeping shadow of war. The villagers have taken refuge in the caves; a series of ancient limestone shelters that wind through the hills like a hidden labyrinth. It is a secret they have guarded fiercely, a lifeline in a time of desperation.

Today, she feels the weight of that secret more than ever. Her thoughts drift to Jack, the British pilot whose crash-landing has turned her world upside down. He is a stranger, yet he has become an unexpected ally, a flicker of light in the encroaching darkness. She had seen him only briefly; his blue eyes filled with a mix of resolve and vulnerability.

In that fleeting moment, a connection ignited, binding us together in this chaotic time. Elena takes a deep breath, stealing herself as she walks toward the entrance of the cave. The air is cool and damp, a welcome relief from the oppressive heat outside. As she steps inside, the flickering glow of lanterns dances along the walls, illuminating the faces of terrified villagers huddling together. Their expressions are a tapestry of fear and hope, woven together by the shared bond of survival. She feels their anxiety seeps into her bones, yet she knows she must remain strong for them. "Signora Santoro!" A small voice calls out from the shadows. It's Marco, a bright-eyed boy of about ten, clutching a ragged toy airplane. His innocent gaze pierces through the gloom, and she kneels beside him, cupping his face in her hands.

"Do not worry, Marco," she assures him, forcing a smile. "We are safe here. The caves will protect us." "But what if they find us?" he whispers, his voice trembling. "What if the Germans come?" Elena's heart aches at his fear. She knows the risks all too well, but she cannot let the darkness of that reality overshadow the flicker of hope she has kindled among them. "We will be ready," she promises. "We have a secret of our own, one they cannot take from us." As she speaks, she catches sight of the adults in the cave, their expressions wary yet attentive. They lean closer, their eyes reflecting a mixture of admiration and desperation. The village's secret lies not only in the caves themselves but in the resilience of its people. They have survived hardships for generations, and now, they must unite once more to withstand this storm. "Gather everyone," she instructs, rising to her feet. "We need to discuss how we can protect our home and ourselves."

The villagers respond to her call, moving closer together. Some hold their children tightly, while others exchange anxious glances. With a deep breath, she begins to outline a plan, drawing from the wisdom of her ancestors. She speaks of the narrow passages within the cave that could serve as escape routes, of the hidden supplies they've managed to stockpile, and the importance of keeping the children safe. As she talks, the tension in the air begins to lift. The villagers nod in agreement, their expressions shifting from fear to determination. They have a shared purpose now, a collective resolve to protect their sanctuary. Elena feels a surge of pride swell within her. This is what it means to be part of a community—to stand together against the tide of despair.

Just as she is about to conclude her plan, the cave trembles slightly, a distant rumble echoing through the stone. The villagers freeze, eyes wide with fear. Elena's heart races, but she forces herself to remain calm. "Stay close," she urges, her voice steady. "Whatever happens, we face it together." They all nod, a silent agreement binding them together. Elena senses their fear, but she also feels the strength of their unity. The village's secret is not merely the caves; it is the loyalty and love they share for one another. Hours pass, and the atmosphere shifts. The rumble of artillery becomes more distant, replaced by the sound of children's laughter echoing through the cave. Marco and a few other children start a game, their spirits lifted by the camaraderie of their small sanctuary. Elena watches them, her heart swelling with a bittersweet feeling. In times of war, joy feels like a precious commodity, and she savours the sight of innocence amidst the chaos. Suddenly, the entrance to the cave darkens as a figure steps inside.

I emerge, with my uniform smudged, and my hair tousled, but there's a spark in my eyes that ignites a wave of relief in Elena. The weight of war momentarily lifts as their gaze's lock. "Is everyone alright?" I ask, my voice a soothing balm in the tense atmosphere. "We are safe for now," Elena replies, stepping closer. "But we must remain vigilant. The Germans could return at any time." I nodded, my expression serious. "I've seen their movements from above. They're tightening their grip on the area. We need to prepare." Elena's heart races at the thought of danger closing in, but she feels a surge of determination. With me by her side, our bond fortified by shared purpose, she knows we can face whatever comes next. We gather the villagers, and together, we begin to formulate a more comprehensive plan. As they strategize, my presence brings a sense of calm amidst the uncertainty. Elena watches me interact with the villagers, my charm and genuine concern, easing our fears. She admires my strength, the way I carry the weight of the world on my shoulders yet still managing to uplift those around us.

In that moment, beneath the Sicilian sky and within the protective embrace of the cave, Elena realizes that her village's secret is not just the caves themselves, but the unyielding spirit of its people—and the love that can blossom even in the darkest of times. Together, it will protect what we hold dear, and she knows that whatever challenges lie ahead, we will face them together. The dust settles in the cave, shrouding the dim light that filters through the rugged entrance. I sit against the cold stone wall, my heart still racing from the crash landing just hours before. The sounds of the village—the muffled cries of children, the anxious whispers of the elders—echo in my ears, blending with the distant rumble of artillery fire.

I glance at the small group of villagers huddled together, their faces etched with worry, their eyes reflecting a mixture of fear and hope. Elena kneels beside a little girl, brushing the dirt from her tear-streaked cheeks. The girl, no more than seven, clutches a ragged doll to her chest, her wide eyes searching for reassurance. I can see the bond forming between them, a silent conversation that transcends words. Elena's gentle touch calms the child, a testament to her strength. It's in moments like this that I realize how desperately these people need a beacon of light amid the shadows of war. I catch Elena's gaze across the cave. She holds my stare for a heartbeat longer than necessary, and in that moment, the world outside fades away. The flickering flames of the small fire cast dancing shadows across her face, illuminating the determination that resides within her. Her eyes, dark and deep, tell stories of resilience and sacrifice—stories I long to know but can't yet understand. It's strange, this shared silence. It binds us together in a way that words cannot. We are both wounded souls in a brutal world, seeking solace in each other's presence.

I feel the weight of her gaze and wonder if she feels the same pull toward me, the same inexplicable connection that compels me to stay close. In this cave, beneath the Sicilian sky, we are just two human beings, grappling with the chaos around us. Elena stands, brushing her hands on her skirt, and moves to the entrance of the cave. The sunlight spills in, brightening the otherwise sombre space. She squints against the brightness, her silhouette framed by the rugged rocks. I admire her bravery; she doesn't shy away from the danger outside but rather faces it head-on. It's a stark contrast to how I feel stuck between fear and the instinct to flee. "Jack," she calls softly, and I rise instinctively, drawn to her side as if by an invisible thread. "Come look. You need to see this."

I join her at the cave's mouth, and together we peer out at the village below. The landscape is both beautiful and haunting. Olive trees sway gently in the breeze, their gnarled branches reaching out toward the azure sky, and the distant sound of laughter carries on the wind. Yet, the remnants of war, a crumbling wall, a charred building, serve as constant reminders of the peril that lingers in the air.

"Do you think they'll come?" she asks, her voice barely above a whisper. I know she's not just talking about the Germans. She's asking about hope, about the possibility of rescue. My heart aches at the weight of her question. "I don't know," I admit, my voice heavy with uncertainty. "But we have to believe they will." She turns to me, her expression resolute. "Believing is all we have right now."

In that moment, I realized that it isn't just her words that inspire me; it was the fire in her spirit. It ignites something within me, a flicker of hope that I didn't know I possessed. We stand together, two solitary figures against a vast and hostile world, and for the first time since my crash, I feel a semblance of peace. As the sun begins its descent, the sky transforms into a canvas of oranges and purples, a breathtaking sight that takes my breath away. I feel the warmth of the light on my face, and it reminds me of home—the sunsets over San Francisco, the sound of the waves crashing against the shore. For a fleeting moment, I forget the war, the fear, and the uncertainty. I am simply a man, captivated by the beauty of the world, standing beside a remarkable woman. "Jack," Elena's voice pulls me back to reality. "We need to figure out a plan. If they come here…" Her voice falters, and I can see the struggle behind her eyes. "We can't let them take this village."

"Then we won't," I reply, my voice firm. "We'll protect them. I'll help you." She turns to me, surprise flickering in her gaze. "You would do that? For us?" "Of course," I say, and mean it. "You've already done so much for me. It's time I repay the favour." Her lips curl into a small smile, and my heart stutters at the sight. It's a smile that holds promise, that speaks of kinship and resolve. Together, we can face whatever comes our way. The shared silence that envelops us once again feels different now charged with a new energy. It's no longer just a silence of fear; it's filled with a sense of purpose, of determination. I can feel the weight of the world pressing down on us, but in this moment, standing side by side, we are not alone. We are united by a shared purpose; a bond forged through the trials that lie ahead. Beneath the Sicilian sky, we find strength in each other, a flicker of light in the encroaching darkness. And as the sun dips below the horizon, I know that whatever challenges await us, I will stand by Elena's side, ready to fight for the hope that has begun to bloom between us.

3

Crossing Paths

The sun hangs low in the sky, casting a golden hue over the uneven terrain of Sicily. I emerge from the shadows of the craggy hills. A warm breeze carries the scent of wild rosemary and distant woodsmoke, I can hear the distant bleat of goats echoing across the valley, grounding me in this rugged land. My heart pounds with a mix of apprehension and hope—each step forward feels heavier with the weight of uncertainty, yet the landscape ahead seems to promise a new beginning. My heart pounds with the intensity of the moment, thrumming like the engine of the fighter plane I once piloted.

The air is thick with dust and the acrid scent of smoke, remnants of the chaos that has turned this idyllic village into a ghost of its former self. I tread carefully, each step fraught with uncertainty, acutely aware that I am a stranger in a land teetering on the edge of despair. As I navigate through the narrow, winding paths, I catch sight of a figure standing a few yards ahead. She is perched on a low stone wall; her silhouette etched against the backdrop of a fading sky. My breath catches in my throat. There's something ethereal about her, a quiet strength that emanates from her very being. The soft curves of her face are framed by dark, cascading hair that dances gently in the breeze. She turns slightly, and I am struck by the deep brown of her eyes, pools of warmth and resilience that seem to pierce through the turmoil surrounding us.

I hesitate, unsure of how to approach her. The language barrier looms like a chasm between us, yet an inexplicable urge compels me forward. I step out from behind the cover of the boulders, the crunch of gravel underfoot announcing my presence. She looks up, her gaze locking onto mine, and for a moment, the world around us fades away. In her eyes, I see a flicker of recognition—perhaps she senses my desperation, the weight of my solitude in this war-torn land. "Hello," I manage to say, my voice a rough whisper. I instinctively raise my hands, palms out, as if to signal peace. The word feels foreign on my tongue, yet I cling to it like a lifeline.

Her expression shifts, a mix of surprise and caution, but she doesn't flee. Instead, she tilts her head, studying me as I study her. A moment stretches between us, charged with unspoken understanding. "Are you... American?" she asks, her accent thick but clear, each syllable carefully articulated. "Yes," I reply, hope igniting within me. "I crashed nearby. I didn't mean to intrude." Her brow furrows, and I see the flicker of fear cross her features. "You are in danger here," she warns, her voice a soft melody, yet laced with urgency. "The Germans patrol these hills." "I know," I confess, the weight of the reality settling heavily on my shoulders. "I need to find a way back to my unit. Can you help me?" For a moment, her eyes darted away, as if contemplating the risks involved in aiding a stranger. I can almost see the gears turning into her mind, assessing the danger, weighing the consequences. But then, she takes a deep breath, and I see the resolve harden in her gaze. "Come with me," she finally says, her voice steady.

Relief floods through me as I follow her. She moves with grace, leading me deeper into the village, the air thick with the scent of earth and wildflowers. We weave through narrow alleys, the sound of our footsteps echoing against the weathered stone walls. I take in the village around us— a place that feels both foreign and familiar, steeped in history and hardship. Children peek out from doorways, their faces painted with curiosity and fear, while the distant echoes of laughter serve as a reminder of the innocence that war has stolen. Elena, I soon learn, is her real name, she glances back at me, her expression softening as she senses my awe. "This village has seen much," she says, her voice barely above a whisper. "We have lived through the darkness. But we must find a way to survive." "Survival is all I can think about right now," I admit, glancing over my shoulder, half-expecting to see the looming figures of enemy soldiers. "I didn't choose to be here, but I'll do whatever it takes."

She nods, her resilience palpable. "As will I," she replies, determination etched into her features. "You are not alone anymore, Jack." The sound of distant explosions echoes in the background, a stark reminder of the chaos outside our fragile bubble. Yet, in this moment, standing in the presence of this extraordinary woman, I feel a flicker of hope. I realize that despite the war raging around us, fate has conspired to bring us together. We arrive at a small schoolhouse, its paint peeling and windows shattered, yet it stands as a testament to the resilience of the village. "This is where I teach," she tells me, her voice tinged with pride. "I want to protect these children, to give them some semblance of normalcy amid the chaos."

I follow her inside, and my heart aches at the sight of the empty classroom, desks arranged in neat rows but devoid of laughter and learning. "You're a teacher?" I ask, admiration creeping into my voice. "Yes," she replies, her gaze drifting over the dusty chalkboard. "But right now, my students are scattered, hiding from the danger. I worry for their safety." "Let me help," I offer, a surge of purpose igniting within me. "I may not be a teacher, but if there's anything I can do…"

Elena's eyes widen in surprise, and then she smiles—a radiant expression that lights up her face. "You would help us?" she asks, her tone laced with disbelief. "Absolutely," I affirm, the weight of my promise settling in my chest. "I may be a soldier, but I want to protect what little hope remains here." She studies me for a moment, and I sense a bond forming, an unspoken agreement that transcends the barriers of language and culture. In that fleeting glance, I see the possibility of something greater, something worth fighting for in this war-torn world.

As we stand together in the hushed silence of the classroom, I realize that this moment marks the beginning of something profound. Beneath the Sicilian sky, amidst the echoes of war, two hearts are crossing paths, bound by a shared purpose and an undeniable connection that neither of us fully understands yet. But in this uncertain world, one thing is clear: we will face the challenges ahead together. The sun filters through the jagged openings of the cave, casting dappled shadows on the rocky floor, illuminating the worried faces of the villagers huddled together. The air is heavy with tension, a palpable reminder of the chaos that reigns just outside their sanctuary. I glance around at the children, their wide eyes reflecting both fear and curiosity. They are too young to understand the full weight of war, yet they sense the urgency of the moment. It is here, surrounded by these frightened souls, that I find myself acutely aware of the barrier between us—a barrier that is not merely physical but also linguistically insurmountable.

Elena stands a few feet away, her dark hair pulled back in a loose braid, her brow furrowed in concentration as she speaks softly to a small girl cradling a doll. "Non avere paura," she reassures, her gentle voice a soothing balm against the harshness of the world outside. I can't understand her words, but the tone is clear—warmth, kindness, and an unwavering resolve. It's a language that transcends mere vocabulary, a language of survival, of humanity. I find myself drawn to her, my heart swelling with an admiration I cannot articulate in words. As the villager's murmur among themselves, I realize I must find a way to communicate—an act of necessity driven by the urgency of our shared plight. I take a deep breath, stepping closer to Elena, careful not to impose upon her moment with the girl. "Elena," I say, the name slipping from my lips with a sense of reverence. She turns to me, her eyes searching for mine, and for a moment, the world around us fades.

"Jack," she replies, her voice a soft melody, even if I only half understand what she means. The sound of my name spoken in her lilting accent sends a shiver down my spine, igniting a flicker of hope amidst the despair. "Can we… talk?" I stammer, gesturing vaguely between us and the villagers. I'm acutely aware of how inadequate my words are. I can feel the weight of my English accent, as if it's a barrier of its own. Yet, I press on. "We need to—" I pause, trying to summon the right words, "—find a way to help them." Elena's expression shifts, a flicker of understanding sparking in her eyes. She nods slowly, and it feels as though we've forged a fragile bridge across our linguistic divide. "Yes," she replies, the word simple yet imbued with a profound sense of agreement. "We must help." With newfound determination, I point to the children, then gesture toward the cave's entrance, indicating the outside world. "They... can't go out there," I say, trying to convey the urgency of our situation. "Danger."

I drew my finger across my throat, mimicking the sound of gunfire in the air, a crude imitation of the violence lurking just beyond the cave's mouth. Elena's eyes widen, and she nods again, understanding the weight of my message. "We need to protect them," she states, her tone resolute. "But how?" It's a question that hangs heavy between us, the enormity of the responsibility settling like a stone in my gut. I think for a moment, considering our options. "Food," I say finally, recalling the meagre rations I had packed in my flight jacket—enough for a few days but not close to sufficient for the group. "We need more food." I look around, hoping to catch the eye of one of the villagers, but they seem too consumed by their fears to notice me. "And... communication," I add. "We need to know what's happening outside."

Elena furrows her brow, clearly wrestling with the same challenges that occupy my mind. "I have a few supplies," she says after a moment, her voice steady. "Some food, from the school." She looks toward the back of the cave, where a large sack rests against the wall, its contents concealed by a dusty cloth. "But we must be careful. If the Germans see us—" I nod, understanding the risk. "We could send someone for help," I suggest, though the thought brings a rush of dread. Sending a villager out into the chaos seems reckless yet staying hidden feels like an equally dangerous gamble. "But who?" Elena's gaze sweeps over the group. "Perhaps the older boys," she proposes, her voice firm. "They can move quietly. We can teach them a few words, so they don't draw attention." "Good idea," I agree, feeling a surge of hope. "And we can use gestures, too." The thought of teaching these boys words and signs fills me with a sense of purpose. It's a small step, but in the face of overwhelming odds, every little bit counts.

Together, we gather the older boys, their faces, a mix of fear and determination. I kneel down to meet their eyes, drawing upon the limited vocabulary I know. "Danger," I say, pointing outward toward the cave's entrance, mimicking the sound of gunfire once more. "You... go. Find food. Help." Elena stands beside me, her presence grounding me as I navigate the challenge of communication. She mirrors my gestures, her hands moving with grace as she emphasizes the importance of silence and caution. "Silenzio," she instructs, her voice gentle yet firm, her gaze unwavering. "If you go, be quiet. Be brave."

The boys nod, their expressions shifting from apprehension to resolve, and I can't help but feel a rush of admiration for their courage. It's a bond forming in the midst of chaos, a language of survival that transcends words. Together, we are building something greater than ourselves—hope. As the boys prepare to leave, I catch Elena's eye again. "We'll be ready," I promise, though the weight of uncertainty lingers between us. "Together."

Her smile is soft, a flicker of warmth against the cold reality of our situation. "Together," she echoes, and in that moment, I know we are forging a connection that transcends the barriers of language—a bond built upon trust, resilience, and the shared desire to protect those we hold dear. As the boys slip out of the cave, I can almost feel the tension in the air begin to ease. The language of survival is not just about words; it's about understanding, about finding ways to connect when the world feels intent on tearing us apart. And as I stand beside Elena, I realize that in this foreign land, beneath the weight of the Sicilian sky, we are no longer just strangers caught in the crossfire of war. We are allies, partners bound by fate, navigating the storm together—one glance, one gesture at a time.

The sun hangs low in the Sicilian sky, casting a warm golden hue across the rugged landscape. The air is thick with the scent of wild herbs and the distant sound of children's laughter echoes through the narrow, winding streets of the village. I find myself leaning against a crumbling wall, watching the villagers scurry about, their faces a mix of worry and determination. My heart races as I think of my mission, my comrades, and the chaos swirling around us. But here, in this moment, I am captivated by something far more profound. Elena emerges from a narrow alley, her dark hair cascading down her back like a waterfall of ink, framing her face in a way that makes my heart skip a beat. She carries a basket filled with freshly baked bread, the aroma wafting through the air and mingling with the salt of the sea. I can't help but admire the way she moves, each step purposeful and graceful, a quiet strength radiating from her. She spots me and offers a tentative smile, her eyes shining with an intensity that seems to pierce through the chaos of war.

"Jack," she says, her voice soft yet firm, as if she's both welcoming and challenging me at once. I respond with a nod, still grappling with the language barrier that separates us. We are two souls caught in a storm, yet here we stand, on the precipice of something unspoken. She approaches, setting the basket down at my feet. "You must eat," she insists, her hands gesturing towards the bread. "It will give you strength." I pick up a loaf, its crust still warm, and tear off a piece. The taste is heavenly, a reminder of the simple pleasures that exist even amidst turmoil. As I chew, I watch her, fascinated by the way her brow furrows in concentration. There's a weight on her shoulders, a burden she carries for her village, and yet she stands before me with an unwavering resolve. "Thank you," I managed to say, my voice a hoarse whisper. It's a small gesture, but in her eyes, I see the flicker of understanding. She nods, and the silence stretches between us, laden with meaning.

We sit together on the weathered stones, the sun dipping further on the horizon, painting the sky in hues of orange and purple. I try to find the words to bridge the gap that divides us, to reach across the chasm of language and culture. "I'm… am English," I say slowly, piecing together simple phrases. "Pilot. Here… for the war." Elena's gaze sharpens, and I can see her processing my words, translating them in her mind. "Pilot," she repeats, her accent thick, but her pronunciation clear. "Flying… in the sky." She gestures upward, her fingers tracing the outline of planes that no longer soar above us, now only memories of freedom and fear.

"Yes," I say, encouraged by her attempt. "But… not safe here." I waved my hand, indicating the village and the distant rumble of artillery. "Danger." Her expression darkens, and for a moment, I see the fear that lurks behind her brave facade. "We are all in danger," she replies quietly, her voice barely above a whisper. "But we are strong. We hide; we protect ourselves. It is what we must do." I feel a surge of admiration for her. She embodies resilience, a quality I've always respected but never truly understood until now. Here she is, a schoolteacher turned protector, navigating a reality that threatens to unravel at any moment. "What can I do?" I ask, wanting to offer my help in whatever way I can. She looks at me, assessing my sincerity, and I hold her gaze steady. "You can help us," she says after a moment. "You can learn our ways.

Understand our fears. Together, we can survive this."

The notion sparks something within me—a sense of purpose beyond the war, a mission that transcends the battlefield. I nod, feeling a deep connection with this woman who has become my unexpected ally. "Teach me," I say earnestly. "Show me how to help." "Words are not enough," she replies, a hint of a smile breaking through her somber expression. "But we will start with small things. I will teach you, our language. It will be a way to connect."

And so, we embark on an impromptu lesson beneath the Sicilian sky, our laughter mingling with the distant sounds of the village. We share simple words— "amore," "libertà," "famiglia"—each syllable a step toward bridging the divide that separates us. It's clumsy at first, my pronunciation awkward, but Elena's patience is infinite. She corrects me gently, her laughter a balm for my insecurities.

With each new word, I feel the distance between us shrink, the walls that language had built beginning to crumble. We talk about life in the village, the children she teaches, the stories she shares, the dreams that flicker like candlelight in the shadows of war. In return, I share tales of my life back home—of wide-open skies, the thrill of flight, and the beauty of dreams untainted by conflict.

As the sun dips lower, casting long shadows, I catch glimpses of Elena's spirit—a passionate teacher, a protector of her people, a woman of indomitable strength. I realize that the war may have brought us together, but it is our shared humanity that binds us. In that moment, beneath the fading light, I vow to do everything I can to protect this woman and her village. I'm just a pilot, but I will be more than that. I will be a guardian, an ally, a friend. The words we share are more than just sounds; they are promises, hopes, and the beginnings of something beautiful.

As the stars begin to twinkle in the darkening sky, I look into Elena's eyes and see a reflection of my own determination. We are bound together by circumstance, by war, but also by an unspoken connection that transcends the chaos around us. I lean closer, feeling the weight of the world fall away, as we take our first steps toward a shared future—one filled with hope, love, and the resilience of the human heart.

4

Crossing Paths

Elena sits on the edge of a weathered stone wall, her fingers tracing the grooves of the ancient rock, worn smooth by time and the elements. As the sun hangs low in the sky, it casts a long shadow that dances over the village. It's a small moment of peace, a fragile pause in a world that has been turned upside down. Just beyond the hills, she knows, the thunder of artillery echoes like a grim reminder of their reality. Her heart is heavy, but there is strength in her resolve. She draws a deep breath, filling her lungs with the scent of wild thyme and salt from the nearby coastline. It grounds her, this connection to the earth, to her people, and to me—the British pilot who crashed into her life like a meteor, bringing chaos but also a flicker of hope. She feels the weight of responsibility pressing against her chest. As the village schoolteacher, she has always been a source of knowledge and guidance for the children, but now her role has shifted. She is not just a teacher; she is a protector, a leader in a time of desperation.

Elena hears the soft rustle of fabric and turns to see me approaching. I walk with a cautious determination, my uniform still bearing the marks of my crash-landing, but there is something different in my gait—an awareness of the danger that surrounds us. My eyes meet hers, and for a moment, the world fades away. She sees the weariness etched on my face, the shadows of conflict lingering in the depths of my gaze. It's a reflection of her own turmoil, and yet, there is a flicker of admiration and warmth that ignites in her core.

"Hey," I say, my voice low, almost hesitant. "How are the children?" Elena smiles, though it doesn't reach her eyes. "They are resilient. Today, they sang songs of hope, voices rising above the fear. They need something to hold onto," she replies, her tone steady despite the anxiety gnawing at the edges of her mind. She knows that hope is as fragile as the petal of a flower, beautiful yet easily crushed.

I nod, my expression shifting from concern to something deeper, a silent acknowledgment of the burden they both carry. "You're doing good work here, Elena. They're lucky to have you." She shakes her head slightly, her heart fluttering at my praise. "I'm just doing what needs to be done. It's my responsibility to keep them safe, to give them a semblance of normalcy. But I worry. What if the next raid comes? What if—" "Stop," I interject gently, stepping closer. "You can't carry all of this alone." My eyes search hers, and she feels the heat of my gaze, a steady anchor amidst the tumult. It's an unspoken recognition that we share this weight, this alliance born out of necessity but deepening into something more profound.

"I don't know how to be brave, Jack," she confesses, her voice barely above a whisper. "I only know that I must be for them." "You're braver than you realize," he reassures her, his voice steady and filled with conviction. "Every day you stand up for them; you fight against the darkness that wants to swallow them whole. That's courage." My words wrap around her like a warm blanket, and she feels the tension in her shoulders ease slightly. It's strange how a simple exchange can feel so significant, how our shared experiences have forged a bond that transcends language and culture. Still, beneath the surface, a storm brews. The weight of the war presses down on them, and she knows that danger is never far away. Elena glances back toward the village, where the children play in the dusty streets, oblivious to the looming threat. "They deserve a future," she murmurs, her heart aching with a fierce love for them. "I can't let them grow up in a world like this. I need to do everything in my power to protect them."

I step closer, my presence a shield against the chaos that swirls around us. "We'll find a way. Together. You're not alone in this fight, Elena." At that moment, she feels a swell of gratitude for me, for this alliance we have formed. In the midst of destruction, I have become her rock, a steadfast presence she never expected. There's something undeniably electric in the air between us, a connection that goes beyond our shared struggle. It's a flicker of something more—an understanding that in this world of uncertainty, we have found solace in one another.

As the sun dips lower, casting a golden glow over the landscape, Elena takes a step closer to me. "I have a plan," she says, her voice gaining strength. "If we can gather the villagers, we can create a network. We can share information, watch for signs of danger. We need to be prepared." My eyes light up with approval. "That's brilliant. I can help with that. I can teach them how to stay safe, how to signal if the enemy is near." Elena nods, feeling the fire of determination ignited within her.

Together, we can forge a path through the darkness. "And we can teach them to be brave, to stand together. If we can instill hope in them, we can fight this war not just with weapons, but with our hearts." My smile breaks through the heaviness that has settled over us, and for a fleeting moment, she can see a young man. I am beneath the weight of the war—a man capable of love, laughter, and dreams. It fills her with a sense of purpose, a renewed commitment to protect not just her pupils, but the fragile bond she shares with me. "Let's gather everyone tonight," I say, my tone resolute. "We'll start our plan." Elena's heart races at the thought of uniting the village, of empowering them to take charge of their future. She feels my presence beside her, strong and reassuring. Together, we stand on the precipice of hope, ready to face whatever comes next.

As the sun sinks below the horizon, she knows the battles ahead will not be easy. But with me by her side, she feels the quiet strength within her rise, ready to challenge the storm that looms. Beneath the Sicilian sky, they will fight—not just for survival, but for a future worth living. The air is thick with tension as I stand in the dim light of the cave, the jagged walls closing in around us. The flickering shadows cast by the small fire we've managed to build dance across Elena's face, reflecting a mixture of fear and determination. She's been the anchor in this storm, a steady presence in a world that feels increasingly chaotic. Trust is a fragile thing, especially in times like these, but somehow, Elena and I have forged a bond that defies the odds.

I can see the worry etched in her brow as she moves closer, adjusting the makeshift bandage on my arm. The pain from my crash-landing has become a dull throb, but it pales in comparison to the weight of what lies ahead. She leans in, her fingers brushing against my skin, and I feel an electric spark course through me. It's a reminder that amidst the destruction, a connection is blossoming between us—one that neither of us expected. "We need to come up with a plan," I say, my voice low but steady. I can't help but admire her resolve. The way her dark hair falls in waves around her shoulders, the way her eyes—deep and expressive—hold a flicker of hope even in the face of despair. "The Germans are tightening their grip. We can't stay here forever." She nods, her gaze unwavering. "I've been speaking to the villagers," she replies, her voice barely above a whisper. "They're scared, Jack. Many are thinking of leaving the caves and returning to the village, but that's a death sentence. If we're caught—"

"We won't be caught," I interrupt, a surge of determination rising within me. "I promise you, Elena. I won't let anything happen to you or the villagers." The words spill out with an intensity that surprises me. The weight of my promise settles over us like a heavy cloak, binding us together in this moment. Elena's lips part slightly, and for a heartbeat, I think she might speak. But then she closes her mouth, her expression shifting as if she's weighing the gravity of my words. Trust is a currency that can be spent easily, but I can see she's discerning, examining the sincerity behind my eyes. "You're risking so much, Jack," she finally says, her voice trembling slightly. "You're a soldier, and I'm just a schoolteacher. You have a duty to your country, and I... I'm just trying to protect my home."

"You are more than that," I reply, my voice firm. "You're a leader to these people, and that requires a strength I've seen in very few. That's why I need you to trust me. We can't fight this war alone, and you know these hills are better than I ever could. Together, we can find a way to keep the villagers safe." She studies me for a long moment, and I can feel the weight of her thoughts pressing against the silence between us. There's a flicker of doubt in her eyes, but I can sense the glimmer of hope trying to break through. "What do you propose?" she finally asks, a hint of curiosity lacing her voice, and I can't help but feel a rush of triumph. "We gather the villagers tonight and come up with a plan. We can create a diversion, draw attention away from the caves while the others make their escape to the nearby hills. The terrain will provide cover, and we can regroup there." The thought of putting my plan into action sends a rush of adrenaline coursing through my veins. I know it's risky, but it feels like our only chance.

Elena bites her lip, the weight of the decision heavy on her shoulders. "What if it goes wrong? What if they catch us?" I step closer, my resolve is unwavering. "Then we fight. We fight for each other, for the people we care about. I won't let fear dictate our actions." I reach for her hand, the warmth of her skin igniting something deep within me. "You've brought me back from the edge, Elena. You've shown me that there's more to fight for than just the war. There's something worth saving, and I can't do this without you." She looks down at our intertwined fingers, the moment stretching between us—timeless and fragile. "You're asking me to trust you with their lives, Jack," she murmurs, her voice thick with emotion. "What if I fail?" "You won't," I promise, my voice steady. "We'll do this together. If we fail, we fail together. But if we succeed, it could mean freedom for everyone here." Finally, she meets my gaze, her eyes fierce and resolute. "Alright, let's do it." The fire crackles softly, and the shadows flicker around us, as if the very world is holding its breath. I can feel the weight of her trust settling between us, a bond forged not just in words but in the very essence of our shared struggle.

As we begin to discuss the details of our plan, I realize that this alliance is more than just a strategy for survival; it's the foundation of something far deeper. Beneath the Sicilian sky, amidst the chaos of war, we are unearthing a connection that transcends the boundaries of our disparate worlds. In each whispered word and shared glance, we are crafting a future that, despite the darkness surrounding us, shines with the promise of hope and love. In that moment, as we map out our course, I understand that trust is not just about believing in each other; it is about embracing the unknown together, facing whatever challenges lie ahead with courage and determination. Together, we are stronger, and with that strength, we will fight—not just for survival, but for a chance at a life worth living. The sun dips low in the sky, casting long shadows across the rugged landscape of Sicily.

The air is thick with the scent of earth and olive trees, mingled with the distant echoes of war. I crouch behind a cluster of rocks, my heart pounding in my chest, each beat a reminder of the precarious situation he finds himself in. He glances over at Elena, who sits opposite him, her dark hair framing her face like a halo against the stark backdrop of the hills. There's a resolute glint in her deep brown eyes, a silent understanding that binds them even in the chaos surrounding them. In the week since they've met, they've grown into an unlikely team. I have learned to rely on Elena's instincts, her ability to navigate the treacherous terrain of both the land and the human heart. She has a way of understanding when it's best to speak and when silence speaks louder than words. Today, they are preparing for a mission—one that could change the fate of the villagers hiding in the caves. The German soldiers have intensified their patrols, and the villagers, already terrified, are starting to lose hope. "We need to gather more supplies," Elena says, her voice barely above a whisper, yet filled with urgency. "If we're going to help them, we can't do it on just the rations we've been hiding."

I nodded, my mind racing through the possibilities. The nearest town is a few miles away—dangerously close to the German encampments—but it's their best shot. "We'll have to be quick," he replies, the weight of their mission settling heavily on his shoulders. "If we can blend in with the locals—" Elena interrupts me, a fierce determination flickering in her gaze. "We can't rely on blending in. We need allies who know the land and the people. We need someone who can help us navigate the risks."

I watch her, captivated by her resolve. The war has stripped away so much—the innocence of our lives, the laughter of children in the streets, the simple joy of a shared meal. But in Elena, he sees a flicker of something profound, a spark of hope that refuses to be extinguished. "Who do you have in mind?" he asks, intrigued. "There's a family on the outskirts of the village," she replies, her brow furrowing in concentration. "The Ferraro's. They've been part of this community for generations. If anyone knows how to evade the German patrols, it's them." I feel a surge of admiration for her knowledge of the village, a testament to her dedication. "Let's go then," he says, pushing himself up from his hiding place, brushing off the dirt from his uniform. "Lead the way." Elena rises, her posture firm, and they move cautiously through the underbrush, their senses heightened. The path is narrow, flanked by wildflowers and the occasional burst of vibrant greenery that seems to defy the desolation of war. As they walk, I steal glances at Elena, her features illuminated by the soft glow of the setting sun. There's beauty in her resilience, a strength that draws him closer, even as danger looms in the distance.

After what feels like an eternity of cautious navigation, they approach the Ferraro home—a modest stone house, its walls weathered but standing firm against the ravages of time. My heart races as they draw near, the reality of their situation crashing down on him. This family could be their lifeline or their undoing. Elena knocks gently on the door, her hand trembling slightly. Moments later, the door creaks open, revealing a middle-aged man with kind eyes and an air of quiet authority. "Elena," he greets, relief washing over his features. "Thank God you're safe." "Marco," she replies, stepping forward to embrace him. I watch, feeling a strange sense of belonging wash over him as the man welcomes them inside. The warmth of the home envelops him, a stark contrast to the coldness of the world outside. Once inside, the atmosphere shifts. Marco's wife, Isabella, joins them, her face etched with worry.

"What brings you here?" she asks, glancing between me and Elena. "You know it's dangerous." "We need your help," Elena states, her voice steady. "The village is losing hope. We need supplies, and we need a plan to keep the villagers safe." Marco's expression becomes serious as he processes her words. "The Germans are tightening their grip. It's risky, but... we cannot abandon our people. What do you propose?" I step forward, eager to contribute. "We can gather food and medical supplies from the market in town, but we'll need someone who knows the back routes to avoid detection. That's where you come in."

Isabella's eyes widen with apprehension, but Marco nods, a hint of a smile breaking through his stoic demeanor. "You're right. We can't let fear paralyze us. If we work together, we have a chance." The four of us huddle around a small wooden table, maps spread out before them. I feel a sense of camaraderie growing, the kind that can only be forged in the fires of adversity. We discuss routes, plans, and contingencies, our voices a blend of urgency and determination. As the night deepens, I realize that we are no longer just strangers thrown together by circumstance; we are a team, united by a common purpose. Elena's hand brushes against mine as we reach for the same point on the map, a spark igniting between us that sends a thrill up my spine. It's a fleeting moment, yet it lingers, a reminder of the connection we share—a bond forged in the midst of chaos. As our plans take shape, I feel a surge of hope coursing through me. We are no longer alone in this fight; we have newfound allies in the Ferraro's, and together, we might just stand a chance against the darkness encroaching

Beneath a Sky of Hope

upon them. The path ahead is fraught with danger, but I know one thing for certain—I will do whatever it takes to protect Elena and the village they've come to love. As they finalize their plans, I catch Elena's eye, and at that moment, beneath the Sicilian sky, he understands that love can thrive even in the most perilous of times.

5

The Enemy's Grip

In the distance a rumble of aircraft engines reverberates through the valleys, sending a shiver down my spine as I crouch beside the crumbling stone wall of the village church. The sun hangs low in the Sicilian sky; it casts long shadows that eerily move across the dirt streets of the village. The air is thick with tension, and I can feel it coiling around my chest, tightening with every passing moment. Elena stands a few paces away; her silhouette framed against the fading light.

She glances back at me, her dark eyes reflecting a mixture of fear and determination. The village is on edge; we have all heard the warnings whispered among the townsfolk—the Germans are advancing, and they will not hesitate to crush any resistance. Our refuge, once a sanctuary, now feels like a ticking clock, each minute bringing us closer to the storm that threatens to engulf us.

I take a deep breath and step closer, my heart pounding in rhythm with the distant drone of the planes. "We need to be ready," I say, my voice low but firm. I can see the resolve in her eyes, but I also catch a flicker of fear. It's an emotion I've grown all too familiar with since landing here, yet I wish I could shield her from it, just as I would protect the villagers huddled in the shadows, their faces drawn and anxious. Elena nods, her hands trembling slightly as she clutches the strap of her satchel. "I've spoken with some of the villagers. They want to fight, Jack. They're tired of living in fear."

I can't help but admire her spirit. It's one of the many things that drew me to her—the way she stands steadfast, unyielding in the face of despair. "Fighting is dangerous, Elena. We need to think this through. If we provoke them, it could mean disaster for everyone." "I know what's at stake," she replies fiercely, her voice stronger than I've ever heard it. "But if we do nothing, we're just waiting to be taken. I can't let that happen." Her conviction ignites a fire within me, and I understand her urgency.

The villagers are not just statistics in a war; they are families, children, and dreams that could be obliterated at any moment. Yet, I also know the reality of war—the unpredictability, the chaos that swallows everything in its path. I hesitate, torn between my duty as a soldier and my desire to protect her and the fragile community that has taken me in. Before I can respond, the sound of heavy boots crunching on gravel reaches our ears, freezing us in place. My breath catches as I glance toward the entrance of the church. A group of German soldiers appears on the horizon, their uniforms stark against the fading light, marching with a determined gait that sends dread pooling in my stomach. "Elena," I hiss, urging her to retreat further into the shadows. She complies, but I see the fight in her eyes—she won't abandon her people easily, and I admire her for it. "We need to hide."

We scramble to the back of the church, pressed against the cool stone walls as the soldiers draw closer. My heart races, and I fight to keep my breathing steady, but the tension is palpable. I can see the villagers peeking from behind their makeshift barricades, their expressions a mix of fear and defiance. The soldiers converge at the church's entrance, their voices harsh and guttural. I can't make out the words, but the tone is unmistakable threatening, demanding. I cast a glance at Elena, and she meets my gaze, her expression a mix of fear and resolve. In that moment, I know we are united in this fight, however perilous it may be. "Stay quiet," I whisper, my voice barely audible. She nods, her eyes wide and focused. I can see her mind racing, strategizing, considering options that I haven't even thought of.

The soldiers begin to search the church, their movements methodically. I can hear the clink of their gear, the rustle of their uniforms as they shift about. They move like predators, and I can't shake the feeling that they are hunting not just for rebels but for any semblance of hope that still resides within these walls. "I'll create a distraction," I whisper suddenly, my heart pounding in my ears. "You stay here. If things go wrong—" "No!" she interrupts, her voice sharp and fierce. "I'm not letting you face them alone. If we're going to do this, we do it together." Her words resonate deep within me, igniting a sense of purpose I hadn't expected to feel. Together. It's a simple word, yet it carries the weight of everything we've been through. I nod, the tension easing just a fraction, and we move silently toward the entrance, our bodies pressed against the cool stone. As the soldiers push deeper into the church, I take a breath, my heart racing. "On three," I whisper, feeling the weight of the moment settle upon us. "One... two... three!" With that, I leap from our hiding spot, charging toward the soldiers with a shout, drawing their attention. "Over here!" I yell, hoping to buy Elena and the villagers a few precious moments. The soldiers turned, startled, their hands moving to their weapons.

"Run!" I shout, and the villagers erupt from their hiding places, rushing toward the back exits, their faces a mix of terror and determination. I can feel adrenaline coursing through my veins as I face the soldiers, my heart thundering in my chest. I'm ready to fight, to protect Elena and the people who have shown me kindness in a world turned dark. The first soldier lunges at me, but I sidestep, my training kicking in as I strike back, adrenaline sharpening my reflexes. The chaos around me is deafening, but I keep my eyes on the soldiers, calculating my moves, desperate to shield Elena from the horror unfolding.

But amidst the clamor and confusion, a gunshot rings out, and time seems to slow. I turn, my heart sinking as I see one of the villagers fall to the ground. The reality of war crashes over me like a wave, relentless and unforgiving. "Jack!" Elena screams, her voice cutting through the chaos. I catch a glimpse of her, fighting her way toward me, the fire in her eyes unwavering even in the face of terror. I want to reach for her, to pull her back to safety, but I know we are in the eye of the storm now. We must fight, together. The enemy's grip tightens around us, but as I stand my ground, I realize that beneath this Sicilian sky, amidst the chaos and despair, something beautiful flickers—a bond forged in fire, a love that defies the darkness. And in that moment, I know that we will not go down without a fight. The air hangs heavy with tension, a thick veil of unease that settles over the village like a shroud. I can feel it in the way the villagers move, their footsteps muted, their voices hushed whispers carried away by the warm Sicilian breeze. It's late afternoon, the sky a bruised shade of purple, the sun dipping low in the west, and as the shadows stretch across the cobblestone streets, I see the fear etched into their faces.

I peer from the entrance of the cave, my heart racing as I take in the landscape, once vibrant and alive, now marred by the spectre of war. The distant rumble of artillery echoes through the hills, a grim reminder of the German forces tightening their grip on the region. They are everywhere, their presence palpable, a dark cloud looming over us. Elena stands beside me, her eyes scanning the horizon, searching for something—hope, perhaps, or a sign that this nightmare will end. I can sense her worry, feel the tension in her posture as she clutches a worn leather satchel to her chest, a talisman of normalcy in these chaotic times. She turns to me, her gaze piercing, and I see the flicker of determination beneath her anxiety.

"Jack," she whispers, her voice barely above a breath. "We can't stay here much longer. They will find us." I nodded, swallowing hard against the lump in my throat. I know she's right. Each day that passes, the danger grows. The villagers rely on us, but I can't shake the feeling that our sanctuary is crumbling. I've seen the fear in their eyes as they gather in the caves, mothers clutching their children, the elderly whispering prayers in the dark. They trust us, but how long can we protect them? The sound of a motorcycle engine revving in the distance sends a jolt of adrenaline through me. I step away from the mouth of the cave, urging Elena to follow. We slip deeper into the shadows, our hearts racing, the air thick with the scent of damp earth and desperation. "Do you think they know?" I ask, my voice low. Elena shakes her head, her brow furrowed. "I... I don't know. But they're searching. I overheard some of the men talking."

Her words hang in the air, heavy with meaning. The whispers of fear are everywhere, creeping into our conversations, our thoughts. The villagers are terrified, afraid that their home—this sacred place—will be stripped from them, that they will be left with nothing. "What did they say?" I press, urgency lacing my tone. Elena hesitates, her eyes darting to the cave entrance before she glances back at me. "They believe there is an American pilot hiding among us. They think he crashed nearby." The weight of her words settles like lead in my stomach. I'm that pilot—an unwitting beacon of hope and danger. I can't let them suffer because of me. "Is there a plan?" I ask, my mind racing. "We need to get them out of here."

Elena nods, her expression resolute. "There's a route through the hills that leads toward the coast. If we can gather the villagers, we might be able to make it there before they close in." The flicker of hope ignites in my chest, but I know the risks. It won't be easy. "What if they spot us? The roads are swarming with patrols." "Then we'll have to be careful. We'll move at night. They won't expect us to flee in the dark." Her voice is steady, but I can see the tremor in her hands. As we strategize, I can't help but admire Elena's strength. She's brave in a way that transcends mere survival; she embodies the spirit of her people, fierce and unyielding. But I can't ignore the fear that gnaws at me. Each decision we make could mean life or death—not just for us, but for the villagers who have taken us in. We steal a glance at the families huddled in the cave, their faces pale, their eyes wide with uncertainty. They cling to their children, whispering reassurances that I know they don't truly believe. In this moment, I wish I could take away their pain, shield them from the horrors that surround us. But I am only a man, a soldier thrust into a war I did not choose.

"Jack," Elena's voice pulls me from my thoughts. "We need to be ready. If we don't act soon, it will be too late." I nod, my resolve hardening. "We'll gather everyone tonight. We'll leave at first light." But as the sun sinks lower, I can't shake the feeling that time is slipping away. The whispers of fear grow louder, echoing in my mind, mingling with the distant sounds of gunfire that punctuate the stillness of the evening. Elena reaches out, her fingers brushing against my arm, grounding me in the present. "We will find a way through this. Together." Her words fill me with a flicker of courage. I look into her eyes, the depth of her determination igniting a spark within me. She believes in us, in our ability to overcome this darkness. As the night descends, we prepare for the journey ahead. The weight of uncertainty hangs over us, but in this moment, beneath the Sicilian sky, I feel a fragile thread of hope weaving through our fears. Together, we will face whatever comes, united in our fight for survival, our hearts beating as one against the encroaching shadows.

The air is thick with tension, a tangible reminder of the chaos that surrounds us. As I crouch against the damp stones of the cave, I can hear the distant rumble of artillery and the echo of footsteps above, a haunting symphony of war that reverberates down into our makeshift refuge. I glance at Elena, whose brow is furrowed in concentration as she sketches something in the dirt with a stick. I can't help but admire her resolve. Even in the face of fear, she remains a beacon of courage, her spirit unyielding. "Jack," she murmurs, her voice barely above a whisper, "we need to come up with a plan." Her dark eyes meet mine, and in that moment, I see a flicker of determination igniting within her. It's a reminder that amidst the horrors unfolding outside, there is still hope—however fragile it may be.

I nodded, the weight of our circumstances settling heavily on my shoulders. The villagers are counting on us, and I can't allow fear to dictate our next steps. "You're right," I reply, my voice steady. "We can't stay here forever. The Germans will tighten their grip on this area, and we'll be trapped." Elena pauses, her gaze drifting toward the cave's entrance, where the flickering light from the outside world casts ominous shadows. She exhales slowly, composing herself. "We should find a way to communicate with the Allied forces. There must be a way to signal for help."

"Do you think the villagers would risk it?" I ask, glancing at the small group huddled nearby. They wear expressions of anxiety, their faces pale and drawn. The children cling to their mothers, eyes wide with fear. The last thing I want is to put them in danger. Elena bites her lip, contemplating the situation. "They are scared, but they also want to fight back. We've been discussing the possibility of creating a diversion—a way to draw attention away from the village."

"A diversion?" I raise an eyebrow, intrigued. "What do you have in mind?" She sits up straighter, her enthusiasm palpable. "If we can gather enough supplies—old boxes, rags, anything flammable—we could create a fire on the outskirts of the village. Something that would make the Germans think we're preparing to defend ourselves here, rather than hiding in the caves." I consider her suggestion, and a sense of admiration washes over me. It's a risky plan, but desperation can inspire ingenuity. "That could work," I say slowly. "But we need to make sure it's big enough to be seen from the air. We also need someone brave enough to light it." Elena nods, her expression resolute. "I can do it. I'll take the risk."

I shake my head, instinctively, protectively. "No. You need to stay here. If something goes wrong—" "But if I don't, we may miss our chance," she interrupts, her voice firm. "We both know that we can't afford to wait any longer. The more time we spend hiding, the more likely it is that we'll be discovered. I run a hand through my hair, frustration bubbling beneath the surface. "You're right, but I can't just sit idly by while you put yourself in danger. I care about you too much to let you risk your life like that." Her eyes soften, and for a moment, the chaos around us fades away. "Jack, I care about you too. But this isn't just about us anymore. It's about everyone in this village. We must do something." Her passion ignites something within me, igniting my own determination. "Okay," I concede, my heart pounding in my chest. "But we'll need more than just a fire. We'll need a signal for the planes. Something that will alert them without drawing too much attention from the Germans." Elena's face brightens on the challenge. "What if we use a mirror or something shiny? If we can catch the sunlight at just the right angle, it might be visible from above."

I nodded, impressed by her resourcefulness. "That could

work. And we can use the fire as a distraction while we signal for help. When the planes see the smoke, they'll know something is amiss and come to investigate." A flicker of hope dances in her eyes. "We'll need to gather the villagers. If we can get everyone on board, we can make this work." With a renewed sense of purpose, I stand, scanning the cave for any potential supplies. "Let's do it, then. We'll gather what we need and start organizing everyone. The sooner we act, the better our chances." Elena rises as well, her spirit infectious. "I'll talk to the women and the children. They want to help; I can sense it. If we can give them a sense of purpose, it might help ease their fears." As we move toward the villagers, I feel an undeniable shift in the atmosphere. The fear that once gripped me loosens its hold, replaced by a fierce determination. Together, we can do this. We can fight back against the tide of despair that threatens to consume us.

Elena's voice calls out to the villagers; her words laced with urgency and strength. I watch as she rallies them, igniting a spark of hope in their eyes. It's in moments like these that I realize how much she embodies the spirit of resilience, the very essence of the Sicilian sky that stretches above us, vast and unyielding. As I join her side, I can't help but feel a surge of admiration. It's not just her bravery that captivates me; it's the way she inspires others to stand tall, to fight for their future. I'm reminded that beneath the weight of war, something beautiful can emerge—an unbreakable bond forged in the fires of adversity.

We may be standing on the precipice of danger, but together, we're crafting a plan, a beacon of hope amidst the shadows. And as I look into Elena's determined eyes, I know that no matter what lies ahead, we will face it together.

6

A Fragile Connection

Elena stands at the edge of the cave, her heart a tempest of emotions, we manage to watch the sun dip below the horizon, bathing the rocky landscape in hues of orange and purple. The shadows lengthen, and with them, the weight of uncertainty settling heavily on her shoulders. She glances back at the villagers huddled together, sharing hushed whispers and anxious glances, their faces painted with fear and hope in equal measure. The children, too, with their wide eyes and unspoken questions, tug at the corners of her heart. Our

Beneath a Sky of Hope

innocence starkly contrasts with the chaos of war that encroaches upon our lives.

I arrive in their village it had been nothing short of a miracle, a bright spark in a time of darkness. I was the embodiment of strength and courage, qualities she admired but also feared. The connection we formed, woven through shared glances and quiet conversations, had bloomed into something beautiful, yet fragile, as delicate as the wildflowers peeking through the cracks in the rocky ground. She feels drawn to me, a magnetic pull that both excites and terrifies me. In his presence, she glimpses a future beyond the war, a dream that feels almost forbidden. But what would that future look like? The war continues to rage, and every day brings fresh horrors, whispers of loss that echo through the village. Could she allow herself to hope for something more than mere survival? The thought sends a shiver down her spine. She knows the cost of attachment, of allowing someone into her heart when the world around us is crumbling. What if I am taken from her, just like so many others? The fear of losing me gnaws at her insides, a relentless ache that she struggles to suppress.

Elena closes her eyes, breathing in the sharp scent of the Mediterranean air, mingled with the earthy aroma of the cave. She can hear my laughter echoing in her mind, a sound so rich and full of life that it feels like an antidote to the despair that lingers in the corners of her heart. She remembers the way I looked at her during those quiet moments, my blue eyes searching for her as if trying to unravel the mysteries held within. In those fleeting seconds, the war faded, and all that existed was an undeniable connection—the promise of something more. But the weight of responsibility bears down on her. She is not just a schoolteacher but a protector of these frightened souls, the children who rely on her for comfort and guidance. They look to her for strength, and she must be their beacon amidst the storm. She cannot afford to be swept away by her feelings for me. To do so would be a betrayal, not only to herself but to everyone who depends on her. As she turns back to the villagers, her heart aches with the burden of her choices.

The children are nestled close to their parents, their small bodies seeking warmth and safety. She feels a pang of longing for that same comfort, but it seems so far out of reach. She watches as a little girl, no older than six, clutches a tattered doll, her wide eyes filled with unshed tears. Elena kneels beside her, brushing a strand of hair behind her ear, offering a gentle smile. "Ciao, piccola," she whispers softly. "Everything will be alright." But even as she speaks those words, uncertainty clings to her like a shadow. Every day, she witnesses the toll the war takes on her people—the fear, the heartache, the loss. How can she promise safety when the world outside their sanctuary is filled with danger? The girl's small hand clutches her own, and for a heartbeat, Elena feels the weight of her own fears dissolve. In that moment, she is a protector, a shield against the darkness. Yet, the moment is fleeting.

My face echoes in her mind again, the way I brush my hands through my tousled hair, my laughter that spills forth when I shared stories of my life back home. She remembers how I spoke of his dreams, of flying above the clouds, of the freedom I craved. She had shared her own dreams too, of a classroom filled with laughter, of children learning and thriving. They shared a vision that extended beyond the immediate turmoil, a flicker of hope in the relentless night. But hope is a dangerous thing in times like these. It can lead to heartbreak, to shattering despair when the inevitable losses come. The thought sends a fresh wave of panic coursing through her veins. How can she reconcile her feelings for me with the reality of their situation? How can she allow herself the luxury of love when the war threatens to pull them apart at any moment?

Elena looks back toward the cave entrance, where the last remnants of sunlight slip away, surrendering the world to darkness. She can feel the weight of my gaze upon her, the way I watch her with an intensity that leaves her breathless. It is both exhilarating and terrifying. She is acutely aware of the danger that lurks outside, but more so, she is haunted by the possibility of what lies ahead—the potential for love, for a life built on dreams they've shared, and the fear of losing it all. With a heavy heart, she turns her back on the villagers, stepping deeper into the cave, where shadows dance like phantoms against the stone walls. She needs to think, to find clarity amid the chaos swirling within her. As she walks, her fingers trace the rough surface of the cave, grounding her in the present, reminding her of her purpose. She cannot lose herself in daydreams when the reality of survival looms so large. Yet, as the darkness envelops her, the flickering ember of connection she shares with me continues to burn brightly, a beacon of hope amidst the fear, a reminder that even in the darkest of times, love can find a way to endure.

The sun dips low in the sky, casting long shadows across the rugged terrain of the Sicilian hills. The air, thick with the scent of wild thyme and the distant echoes of artillery, seems to hold its breath as if waiting for something to unfold. I sit on a weathered stone, my back against the cool rock, stealing glances at Elena as she kneels on the ground, tending to a small makeshift garden of herbs. Her fingers, delicate yet calloused, dug into the earth with a tenderness that belies the chaos surrounding us. As I watch her, I'm struck by the way she navigates the wilds with an unyielding grace. Despite the grim realities of war, she finds beauty in the simplest of things—a sprouting basil seed, the fluttering of a butterfly, the laughter of children playing in the distance. I can't help but admire her resilience, her ability to find glimmers of hope in our bleak existence. She looks up and meets my gaze, and in that moment, the world around us fades away.

"Jack?" Her voice is soft, yet it carries a weight that draws me in. "Do you think we'll ever get out of here?" The question hangs in the air, heavy with unspoken fears. I want to reassure her, to tell her that the war will end, that the skies will clear, but the truth is elusive, like a shadow slipping through my fingers. Instead, I offer her a small smile, hoping to reflect the flicker of strength I see in her. "Soon, I hope," I respond, my voice steady despite the uncertainty gnawing at my insides. "We just need to keep our heads down and wait for the right moment."

Elena nods, her brow furrowed in thought. She brushes a stray hair behind her ear, and I catch a glimpse of vulnerability in her expression. It's a reminder that beneath her fierce exterior lies a heart that aches for safety, for normalcy, for a life free from the relentless grip of war. "Sometimes, I think about my students," she muses, her eyes drifting toward the horizon. "They're so young, yet they've been forced to grow up in a world filled with fear. I wish I could protect them from all of this."

Her words resonate deeply within me. I think of my own younger siblings back home, their laughter, a distant memory now overshadowed by the grim realities of war. "You're doing more than you realize, Elena," I reply, my voice firm. "By being here for them, you're offering them hope. You're a light in this darkness." A faint blush colors her cheeks, and she looks down, her fingers idly twisting a sprig of rosemary. "Sometimes, I feel so powerless," she admits, her voice barely above a whisper. "What can one person do against an army?" I shifted closer, compelled to bridge the distance between us. "You're not just one person. You're a teacher, a protector, a voice for your village. You give them a reason to believe in tomorrow."

Beneath a Sky of Hope

Her gaze meets mine, and for a moment, the weight of our circumstance's lifts, replaced by an unspoken understanding. We are two souls caught in a storm, yet somehow, we find solace in each other. In this fragile connection, I see the flicker of something deeper, something that transcends the chaos of war. "I've never met anyone like you, Jack," she confesses, her voice barely a whisper. "You carry a strength that inspires those around you." A warmth spreads through my chest at her words. "And I've never met anyone as brave as you," I reply, my gaze steady. "You're fighting your own battles every day, and it takes incredible courage to stand tall in the face of such fear." Elena lowers her eyes, a shy smile playing on her lips. The vulnerability that had once clouded her expression is replaced by a spark of determination. "We must keep fighting, then. For the village, for the children, and for each other." As the sky deepens into dusk, the first stars begin to twinkle overhead. The village is cloaked in a serene silence, interrupted only by the distant rumble of gunfire, a reminder of the world we inhabit. Yet, within this moment, the fear that typically gnaws at my insides is momentarily quieted by the bond we share.

"Tell me about your home, Jack," she says, her voice softening. "What was it like before all of this?" I take a deep breath, allowing memories to wash over me. "It's a small town in Texas, nestled between rolling hills and sprawling fields. We had a big oak tree in our backyard where I played as a kid. My father would take me fishing at the river, and my mother made the best apple pie you could imagine."

As I speak, I can see the picture forming in her mind—my childhood painted with vibrant colours, a stark contrast to our current reality. "What was your favourite part of those days?" she asks, her eyes wide with curiosity. I chuckle softly, feeling the warmth of nostalgia. "Probably the summer nights. We'd sit outside, watching the fireflies dance in the air, and my siblings would run around, chasing after them. It felt so carefree, so… normal." Her smile is bittersweet, a reflection of the world we've both lost. "Normal seems like a distant dream now," she murmurs, a hint of sadness lacing her words. "But it's not gone forever," I insist, my heart pounding with the urgency of my conviction. "We must believe it can return. We have to hold on to those dreams, even in the darkest of times." Elena's gaze intensifies, as if searching for something within my words. "You're right, Jack. Hope is what keeps us alive, isn't it?" In that moment, I realize that our connection isn't merely a refuge from the war—it's a lifeline. Beneath the Sicilian sky, amidst the chaos and fear, we find strength in each other, a fragile yet undeniable bond that fuels our resolve to fight for a better tomorrow.

As the stars twinkle above us, I reach out, gently clasping her hand. The warmth of her touch sends a jolt of electricity through me, a promise that even in the harshest tempest, love can blossom, fragile yet fierce, beneath the very sky that threatens to tear us apart. The sun hangs low in the Sicilian sky, casting a golden hue over the scattered remnants of the village. I stand at the edge of the cave, the cool stone pressing against his back. Beneath the surface, he feels the warmth of the people sheltering within—fear and hope intertwined, like the wildflowers blooming defiantly in the cracks of the earth. Elena kneels on the ground, fingers deftly weaving together strands of straw, creating makeshift toys for the children huddled nearby. Her laughter, soft and melodic, dances through the air, a stark contrast to the distant rumble of artillery.

I watch at her, captivated by her spirit which remains unbroken, even in the shadow of war. He feels an urge to protect that light, to shield her from the darkness encroaching upon their lives. "Here, this one is for you," she says, handing a small figure—a rough representation of a soldier—to a wide-eyed boy. The child's face brightens, momentarily forgetting the chaos outside. I know that these moments are fleeting, yet they are the essence of what he has come to cherish. It is in this fragile connection with Elena and the villagers that he finds purpose amid the turmoil. As the children play, I move closer to Elena, drawn by an invisible thread. She glances up, her eyes meeting mine, and for a heartbeat, the world falls away. There is an understanding that transcends words, a shared burden that binds them even tighter than the threat of the enemy outside. I clear my throat, searching for the right words, but they elude him. Instead, he reaches out, brushing her hand with his, a silent promise of solidarity.

"Do you think they'll come for us?" he asks, his voice barely above a whisper. The air is thick with unspoken fears, and he feels the weight of her gaze as she contemplates his question. "I don't know," Elena replies, her voice steady yet laced with uncertainty. "But we have to be ready, Jack. For the children, for the village… for ourselves." There's a fierceness in her tone that ignites something within him—a determination to stand tall amid the encroaching storm. In that moment, they share a fragile connection, a bond forged not through grand gestures or declarations of love but through quiet resilience and mutual respect. I admire her strength, the way she embraces her role as a protector, and it pulls at his heartstrings. I wonder if she knows how deeply she has affected me, how her bravery has ignited a fire in his soul that he thought had long since extinguished. The sound of distant gunfire echoes through the hills, a grim reminder of the reality they face. My thoughts drift to his fellow pilots, the comrades he had trained with, each of them filled with dreams of glory and honour. I never anticipated this—being stranded in a foreign land, fighting not just for his country but for the very lives of those around him. My heart races, not from fear, but from the weight of responsibility that settles on his shoulders.

I watch as Elena stands, her posture straightening, a woman transformed by the circumstances. She raises her chin and looks out toward the horizon, where the sun dips lower, a fiery orb on the edge of the world. "Whatever happens, Jack, we will face it together," she declares, her voice steady and resolute. "Together," he echoes, the word reverberating between them. And in that simplicity lies everything they have fought for—their lives, their dreams, and the burgeoning love that quietly rises amid the chaos. I reach for her hand once more, this time intertwining our fingers. The warmth of her skin against mine sends a jolt of electricity through me, grounding him in this moment.

I see the flicker of uncertainty in her eyes, a reflection of my own fears, but there's also a spark of something else—a fierce determination to survive, to protect what we have built together. As the shadows lengthen, we huddle closer to the children, sharing stories and laughter, building a fortress of warmth against the cold reality outside. I listen intently as Elena recounts tales of Sicilian legends, her voice animated and full of life. The children lean in, captivated by her words, and for a fleeting moment, the weight of the world lifts, replaced by innocence and wonder. But I can't ignore the gnawing unease in my gut. The enemy is closing in, and with each day passing, the stakes grow higher. He glances at Elena, whose smile is a beacon of hope, and he realizes that this fragile connection they share is more than just survival, it's a lifeline. She has become his anchor, and he is determined to be hers. "Tell me about your life before the war," I urge, desperate to know the woman behind the strength. I crave the details, the richness of her past, to understand the tapestry of experiences that have shaped her.

Elena pauses, her expression contemplative. "I was a teacher," she begins, her gaze drifting as if she can still see the classroom filled with eager faces. "I loved guiding the children, watching them learn and grow." There's a softness in her voice that pulls at his heart. "But now... now everything feels different." "Different how?" he prompts gently, and she meets his gaze, a flicker of vulnerability shining through.

"Now, every lesson feels like it must be about survival," she admits. "I find myself teaching them not just to read and write, but how to find hope in the darkest of places. Her words resonate deeply within him, and he realizes that they are both teachers in their own right—learning from each other, from the struggles they face, and from the love that blooms amidst uncertainty. As the sun dips below the horizon, casting long shadows in the cave, I know that whatever tomorrow brings, this moment, this fragile connection, will be etched in his heart forever. It is a testament to their courage, their resilience, and the unyielding spirit of love that can flourish even in the most desperate of circumstances. I squeeze her hand, and she squeezes back, a silent vow that they will face whatever comes together—bound not just by circumstance, but by an unbreakable bond forged in the fires of war and the light of love.

7

Tempests of War

A palpable weight hangs over the village, as if the tension itself were the dark clouds gathering on the horizon. I stand at the mouth of our hidden refuge, the cool stone pressing against my back, my heart racing as I gaze skyward. The sun, usually a warm companion, now casts an eerie glow, transforming the azure sky into a canvas of foreboding oranges and deep reds. I can feel it in my bones, the storm is coming, and with it, the fury of war. Above me, the distant rumble of aircraft engines grows closer, an unsettling symphony of chaos that sends shivers down my spine. I close my eyes for a moment, trying to steady my breath, to ground myself in the reality of the moment. But it's a futile effort; the memories of the last few weeks flood back—my laughter, the stolen glances that lingered just a heartbeat too long, and the way his presence has become a lifeline in this tumultuous sea of uncertainty.

I hear a soft rustling behind me, and I turn to find Elena,

her expression a mixture of resolve and fear. Her hands tremble slightly, but her eyes are fierce, the fire within them ignited by the resolve to protect her people. I can't help but admire her—this woman who has taken on the weight of the world, who has become a beacon of hope in the darkest of times. She steps forward, her voice barely a whisper, but it carries the strength of a thousand warriors. "Jack, we must find shelter. They'll be here soon." I nod, knowing she's right. The distant hum grows louder, a haunting prelude to the violence that is about to rain down upon us. I glance back at the villagers huddled in the makeshift caves, their faces etched with fear and uncertainty. Children clutch their mothers, eyes wide and searching, while the older villagers whisper prayers, their hands trembling as they grip rosaries.

"Let's go," I say, my voice steady despite the storm brewing both outside and within. I lead Elena deeper into the cave, where the coolness envelops us like a shroud, and we're momentarily shielded from the chaos above. But the walls feel too close, the shadows too deep, and I can sense the unease radiating from everyone around us. We crouch together, a small group gathered close, our breaths held in a fragile silence. The tension is electric, and I can't shake the feeling that the world outside is about to erupt. I can't bear the thought of what might happen to us, to her. I reach out, my hand finding hers, and for a fleeting moment, the chaos of war falls away, leaving only the warmth of our connection. Suddenly, the sky splits open with a deafening roar, and I know, this is it. The aircraft, with its dark silhouettes against the fiery backdrop of the sun, scream overhead, their engines drowning out the sound of my heartbeat. I pull Elena closer, shielding her with my body, the primal instinct to protect surging through me. We exchange a glance, and in that moment, I can see the fear mirrored in her eyes, but also something else, a fierce determination. She's ready to face whatever comes, and so am I.

The first explosion rocks the ground beneath us, a violent tremor that sends dust and debris cascading from the cave's mouth. The villagers cry out, a chorus of panic that rises above chaos. I feel Elena's grip tighten around my hand, her knuckles white as we brace ourselves against the onslaught. "Stay close!" I shout, though I know my voice is barely audible over the cacophony. "We have to stay together!" The bombs fall like rain, each explosion shaking the earth and rattling the very foundations of our refuge. I can hear the screams of the villagers, the sharp cries of children, the desperate prayers spilling from trembling lips.

Beneath a Sky of Hope

The weight of fear presses down on me, and I fight against the urge to succumb to despair. I can't let that happen—not now, not when we've come so far. "Jack!" Elena's voice cuts through the noise, urgent and full of command. "We need to help them!" She's right. The instinct to protect those around us ignites a fire within me, and I nod, determination flooding my veins.

I turn to gather the villagers, to rally them together, but the chaos is overwhelming, and I can feel the walls of the cave closing in—both physically and metaphorically. "Stay calm!" I call out, my voice rising above the din. "We can make it through this. Just hold on!" Elena moves beside me, her presence a steadying force against the storm. Together, we urge the villagers to form a chain, to pass supplies and comfort one another in this crucible of fear. It's a small act, but it feels monumental in the face of the destruction raging outside.

As the explosions continue, I steal glances at Elena—her face lit by the flashes of light from above, her eyes fierce and unwavering. Each time our gazes lock, I can feel the connection between us strengthen, forged in the fires of adversity. I know then that no matter what happens, we are fighting for each other, for the life we've begun to build amidst the ruins.

The sound of a loud crash reverberates through the cave, and I instinctively pull Elena closer, shielding her from the falling debris. "Stay down!" I shout, as a cloud of dust envelops us, choking the air and leaving us gasping. In that suffocating darkness, I realize that our survival hinges not just on evading the bombs but on the unbreakable bond we've formed. It's as if the sky itself is ablaze with our shared resolve, illuminating the path through the chaos. And beneath that fiery expanse, I know we'll find a way, together, to escape this tempest of war. The air around me crackles with uneasy tension, thick and laden with the scent of smoke and fear. I stand amidst the remnants of what was once a bustling village, now reduced to echoes of laughter and the soft whispers of children long gone. The sun hangs low in the Sicilian sky, casting a golden hue over the craggy hills, but the beauty of the landscape feels like a distant memory, overshadowed by the grim reality of war.

I clutch the worn leather strap of my flight jacket, the fabric cool against my palm. Just days ago, I was soaring above these hills, my heart racing with the thrill of flight, oblivious to the chaos brewing below. But now, grounded by circumstances beyond my control, I find myself grappling with a reality that threatens to swallow me whole. My mission to gather intelligence on enemy movements has turned into something far more perilous—an urgent struggle to protect the very people I had hoped to help.

Elena's presence lingers in my mind like a gentle beacon, her strength a stark contrast to the turmoil around us. I can still see her face, illuminated by the dim light of our hidden refuge, her eyes filled with determination and an unwavering spirit. Yet, as I prepare to step into the fray, I can't shake the sense of dread that clutches at my chest. What if I fail her? What if my courage isn't enough to shield her from the horrors that encroach upon us?

The distant rumble of engines breaks my reverie, and I snap back to reality, my heart pounding in rhythm with the approaching threat. I gather the small band of villagers who have chosen to stand alongside me—men and women driven not by a desire for glory, but by a fierce love for their homeland and their families. They look to me for guidance, their faces etched with worry, but also a flicker of hope. I swallow hard, willing myself to be the leader they need. "Listen up," I say, my voice steady despite the tremors of fear coursing through me. "We don't have much time. The Germans are patrolling the area, and we need to move quickly. Our best chance is to create a diversion." I glance around at the faces of the villagers, their expressions a mix of uncertainty and resolve. "I'll draw their attention while you get the children to safety. Once you're clear, I'll follow."

An elderly man steps forward; his brow furrowed with concern. "Lieutenant, it's too dangerous. You're one man against a battalion. We cannot ask you to risk your life for us." The weight of his words settles heavily on my shoulders, but I refuse to back down. "You're not asking me. I'm choosing this. I owe it to you, to Elena. We've fought too hard to let fear dictate our actions. If I can buy you even a few minutes, it could mean the difference between life and death." They exchange glances, silent conversations passing between them—a shared understanding that resonates through the heavy air.

I can see the flicker of resolve igniting in their eyes, and it strengthens my own. "Very well," the old man concedes, his voice hoarse but firm. "We will follow your lead but promise us you will return." I nod, but the weight of that promise hangs heavily on my heart. What if I don't return? The thought sends a chill down my spine, but I shake it off. I can't afford to dwell on what-ifs. The children need their teachers, their parents, their futures. And I need to fight for mine—and for Elena. As I step away from the group, I take a moment to steal my resolve. The village is eerily quiet, the stillness broken only by the rustling of leaves and the distant sound of engines drawing nearer. I can feel my pulse quicken, adrenaline surging through my veins like wildfire. With one last look at the villagers, I breathe deeply, focusing on the task ahead. I'm not just fighting for survival; I'm fighting for love, for a connection that has transcended the chaos of war. I can't let Elena down. Not now.

I slip into the shadows of the trees lining the outskirts of the village, my heart racing as I scan the horizon. The German patrols are closing in, their vehicles rumbling ominously against the gravel road. I grip the handle of my sidearm, my fingers trembling slightly. I have trained for moments like this, but nothing could prepare me for the reality of facing down the enemy.

The first vehicle appears, a hulking mass of steel and menace. I wait, my breath shallow, heart pounding like a war drum. As it approaches, I step into the open, my hands raised in a gesture of surrender. The soldiers inside halt abruptly, their eyes narrowing as they assess the situation.

"British!" one shouts, his voice laced with contempt. "You should have stayed in the sky, Archer!" "Hey!" I call out, trying to keep my tone steady, a façade of confidence masking the storm brewing within. "Looking for a fight? Because I'm right here!" They emerge from the vehicle, rifles at the ready, and I take a step back, feigning vulnerability. "You want a target? I'm all yours."

The soldiers exchange glances, their initial surprise quickly morphing into predatory glee. They move toward me, cocky and confident, but I have something they don't—resolve. As they draw closer, I turn and bolt into the nearby thicket, the sound of gunfire erupting behind me. The bullets whiz past, narrowly missing me as I weave through the trees, adrenaline propelling me forward. I can't think about the odds or the danger; I can only focus on the mission at hand. My heart races as I hear the soldiers pursuing me, their shouts echoing through the woods. I push myself harder, willing my legs to move faster, fuelled by the thought of Elena and the promise I made to return. I can't let anything, or anyone, stand in the way of that hope. I reach a clearing and glance back, spotting a group of soldiers fanning out behind me. I take a breath and push through the brush, my surroundings fading into a blur of green and brown. I can't falter now, not when every second counts.

Suddenly, a sharp pain erupts in my shoulder, and I stumble, falling to the ground. I grit my teeth against the pain, forcing myself to rise. I can't let them win; I can't let them take me down. My vision blurs, but I fight against it, pulling myself up and sprinting once more, the burning ache in my shoulder igniting a fierce determination within me. I push forward, driven by the thought of Elena, her laughter, and the warmth of her smile. I can't let the war consume us. I won't give in to despair. Not now. Not ever. As I reach the outskirts of the village, I hear the distant cries of children, and it fuels my resolve further. I'm not just fighting for my life; I'm fighting for the life I hope to build beyond the ruins of this war. I can see the shelter where the villagers have taken refuge, and I sprint toward it, knowing that I must reach them—before it's too late.

The air crackles with tension as the distant rumble of thunder mingles with the ominous sound of aircraft engines overhead. I stand at the mouth of the cave, my heart pounding in sync with the distant explosions that reverberate through the hills. The night is darker than usual, the Sicilian sky cloaked in heavy clouds, shrouding the moon and stars. I can feel the weight of fear pressing down on me, but I refuse to yield to it. I glance back at Elena, who is crouched among the frightened villagers, her eyes wide with concern as she absorbs the chaos unfolding just beyond our sanctuary. "We can't stay here," I say, my voice low but urgent. "We need to find a way out before they find us." Elena looks up, her expression a mixture of defiance and fear. "And go where, Jack? There's nowhere safe anymore. The Germans are everywhere." Her voice trembles slightly, but I can see the spark of determination in her eyes, the same strength that first drew me to her when I crashed into this world. I step closer, lowering my voice further so only she can hear. "There's a path I noticed on my way here, a way that might lead us to the coast. If we can get there, we can find a boat and—" "Risking our lives for a chance?" she interrupts, her gaze unwavering. "What if it's a trap? What if we run into more soldiers?"

I take a deep breath, trying to quell my rising frustration, knowing that my words must convince her. "Elena, staying here is a death sentence. We must take the chance. We can't let fear dictate our lives. We owe it to ourselves—" "To whom?" she snaps, her voice rising. "To the villagers? You think they'll be safe if we leave? We can't abandon them, Jack!"

The weight of her words settles on my shoulders. I look around at the faces of the villagers, their expressions a mirror of Elena's fear and loyalty. They trust her; she is their beacon of hope. I take a step back, realizing that the path I envision is not just about escape but about survival for all of us. "What if we can help them? If we can reach the coast, we could bring back help. We could—" "Help?" Elena's voice softens but remains steady. "We can't promise them anything. We're all scared and lost. They need us here as much as we need them." I pause, weighing her thoughts against the growing urgency in my chest. The sound of planes grows louder, and I know time is slipping away. "Then let's take them with us. If we leave now, we can get there safely. We can do this together." Elena studies me, her brow furrowed as if she's searching for something in my eyes, faith, courage, or perhaps a shared dream of freedom. "And if we can't?" she asks, her voice barely a whisper. "What if we lead them into more danger?" I reach for her hand, feeling the warmth radiating between us despite the cold grip of terror surrounding us. "We will find a way, Elena. Trust me." After a long moment, she nods, albeit reluctantly, and I can see her resolve solidifying. "Okay. But we do it together, for them."

I glance at the villagers, many of whom are huddled close,

whispering prayers and clutching one another. My heart aches for their plight, but I know that we must act now. "Gather what you can carry. We'll leave in five minutes." As Elena spreads the word, I take a moment to steal myself for what lies ahead. The tension in the air thickens, and I can almost taste the fear mingling with the dust of the cave. I steal a glance outside; the landscape shrouded in darkness and uncertainty. The enemy is closing in, and I can feel the weight of my duty pressing against me. I cannot fail them. Not now. When the time comes, we gather in a tight formation, the villagers—old and young, mothers clutching their children—looking to us for leadership. Elena stands beside me, her presence a steadying force. "Follow closely," I instruct, my voice firm. "Stay quiet and keep moving."

We slip out of the cave into the night, the air thick with the scent of damp earth and impending rain. The clouds above roll ominously, mirroring the turmoil within. I lead the way, keeping my senses alert for any sign of danger. My heart races with every step, knowing that the sounds of war are drawing closer. As we traverse through the dense underbrush, I feel Elena's hand clasping my arm, her grip, a reminder of the hope we cling to. "Jack," she whispers, her voice barely audible above the rustling leaves. "What if they find us?" I turn to look into her eyes, and in that moment, I see the vulnerability she tries to mask. "Then we fight," I reply, my voice resolute. "Together." The path is narrow, winding through the dense Sicilian hills, the shadows dancing like ghosts around us. Every crack of a twig beneath our feet feels like a gunshot in the stillness. I can hear the faint echo of voices in the distance, German soldiers patrolling the outskirts, and I know we must hurry. Suddenly, a loud explosion erupts in the distance, shaking the ground beneath us. The villagers gasp, panic surging through our group. "Keep moving!" I urge, pushing forward as the sound of gunfire mixes with the thunder rumbling above us.

As we reach a clearing, I catch a glimpse of the coast shimmering faintly in the moonlight. Hope ignites within me, but it is quickly snuffed out as I hear the unmistakable roar of engines approaching. I turn back to the villagers, urgency burning in my veins. "This way!" I shout, leading them toward the cover of a thicket. We duck low, hearts pounding as the planes pass overhead, their shadows darkening the ground as they scour the area below. I watch as Elena pulls a small child close, whispering soothing words despite her own fear. The sight of her strength fills me with admiration; she is the heart of this makeshift family we've formed amid the chaos.

After what feels like an eternity, the planes finally disappear into the distance. I motion for everyone to remain still, my instincts on high alert. We've come too far to fail now. As we press forward, the distant sound of waves crashing against the rocks fuels my determination. We're close. But just as we reach the edge of the tree line, the unmistakable sound of footsteps approaches. I freeze, holding my breath as I scan the area. My pulse quickens, my mind racing with thoughts of what could come next. The villagers cluster behind us, fear evident in their wide eyes. "Elena," I whisper, turning to her, "we may have to fight." She nods, her resolve unyielding. "Whatever it takes." And at that moment, beneath the Sicilian sky, amidst the tempest of war raging around us, I knew that together, against all odds, we would seize our chance at freedom.

8

Shelter In the Storm

The air hangs heavy with the scent of damp earth and wild herbs, mingling with the distant drip of water echoing through the darkness, the rough stone walls brush against my fingertips as Elena leads me into through the narrow passageway of the cave. Each step sends my heart pounding with a mix of anticipation and unease, the cool air prickling my skin as shadows flicker along the jagged walls, making the environment feel both claustrophobic and strangely protective. The flickering light of a single oil lamp casts wavering shadows on the rough stone walls, creating an almost surreal atmosphere. She glances back at me, her heart pounding not just from the fear of discovery but also from the undeniable connection that has been growing between us since that fateful day in the village. "Here," she whispers, stepping aside to reveal a small alcove. It's a cozy nook nestled into the cave's contours, shielded from the prying eyes of any soldiers who might wander too close.

A tattered blanket lies folded in one corner, alongside a few meagre supplies, crusts of bread, a jar of olives, and a sloshing bottle of homemade wine. "This is…" she starts, her voice with surprise, "amazing." "Not much," I reply, a hint of a smile gracing my lip as I gesture toward the meagre offerings, "But it's safe. For now." She helps me to set the oil lamp down on a flat rock and takes a moment to catch her breath. The weight of our reality sits heavy upon her shoulders, yet in this small space, surrounded by the echoes of the cave, a sense of sanctuary wraps around us like a warm embrace. I gaze around the alcove, taking in every detail—the way the walls glisten from moisture, the soft rustle of the wind outside, the distant sounds of the village as life continues despite the chaos beyond. "You've made it a home," I observe, my voice low and earnest. Elena feels a blush rise to her cheeks at my compliment. "It's more of a refuge," she replies softly, crossing her arms. "We all do what we can to survive."

I nod, and the silence between us stretches, filled with unspoken thoughts and emotions. She can see the flicker of determination in my eyes, a glimmer that reassures her that they are in this together. "What about the children?" I ask, breaking the silence. "Are they safe?" Elena's heart tightens at the thought of her students—innocents caught in the crossfire of a war they don't understand. "They're hiding with their families," she assures me, her voice steady despite the weight of her worry. "I've been teaching them what I can, but their safety comes first. We all have to look out for one another." I stand a little taller, my shoulders back happy to know that the mention of her students are safe. "And you're doing an amazing job. I've seen how they look at you." The sincerity in my words washes over her like a gentle tide, and for a moment, the weight of the war feels lighter. "They inspire me," she admits, her eyes sparkling with unbidden passion. "Their laughter, their hope... it's what keeps me going."

In the flickering light, I step closer, the space between them narrowing. "And what keeps you going in moments like this?" I ask softly, my voice a low rumble that sends a shiver down her spine. Elena meets my gaze, a rush of emotions surging within her—fear, longing, and an unexpected warmth. "I suppose it's the thought of a better tomorrow," she replies, her voice barely above a whisper. "That there's still beauty in this world, even amidst the darkness." I nod thoughtfully, the shadows dancing on my face. "You're stronger than you realize, Elena. The way you care for your village..." I pause; my expression is growing serious. "You're a beacon of hope for them, just as you are for me." Her heart swells at my words, and she feels a flicker of something deeper ignite within her longing for connection that goes beyond mere survival. The intimacy of the moment wraps around us, and for the first time, she allows herself to imagine a life beyond the confines of war, a life where love can flourish amidst the ruins.

But then, reality crashes in, pulling her back to the present. "We can't stay here for long," she says, her voice steadying.

"We need to keep moving, find a way to help those who can't hide." My expression darkens, a flicker of worry crossing my features. "We'll find a way," I reassure her, determination etched into my voice. "I won't leave you—or them—behind." Elena feels a rush of gratitude swell within her; a bond forged through shared fears and relentless hope. "Thank you, Jack. For everything." I give her a soft smile, and in that moment, the world outside fades away. The chaos of war feels distant, as if they are suspended in time, surrounded only by the warmth of each other's presence. But the moment is fleeting; they both know it. Outside, the distant rumble of explosions reverberates through the cave, shattering their fragile peace. Elena's heart races, and she glances toward the cave entrance, her mind racing with thoughts of what lies beyond.

"Stay close to me," I murmur, grounding her in the moment. I step beside her; my presence is a reassuring force against the uncertainty swirling around us. As we huddle together in the small alcove, Elena feels the weight of the world pressing down on us, yet within this sanctuary, she understands that they have created something beautiful amidst the chaos. Here, beneath the Sicilian sky, in the depths of the earth, we have found shelter—not just from the storm outside, but in each other's hearts. And as the sounds of war continue to echo around them, she knows that whatever comes next, we will face it together. The echoes of distant explosions reverberate through the craggy landscape, a constant reminder of the chaos that engulfs Sicily. Inside the cave, the air is thick with tension, punctuated only by the hushed whispers of the villagers huddled together.

The flickering light from a few hastily arranged candles dances on the stone walls, casting long shadows that seem to stretch towards the corners of the cave, as if trying to escape the reality outside. Elena sits close to me, our shoulders nearly touching, both seeking solace in the presence of each other. The warmth radiating from my being is a comfort amidst the cold dread that wraps around our hearts. She steals a glance at my profile, the sharp line of my jaw is illuminated by the soft glow, and she feels a rush of gratitude for the man who has unexpectedly become her shield against the horrors that plague us.

"Do you think they'll come for us?" she asks, her voice barely above a whisper, trembling slightly as she speaks. The question hangs in the air, heavy and foreboding, and I turn my head slightly to meet her gaze. "I don't know, Elena," I reply, my voice steady, but she can hear the uncertainty beneath my calm exterior. "But we have to believe they will. We can't give up hope." She nods, though uncertainty gnaws at her insides. It's strange how quickly fear can seep into the cracks of one's heart, how it can turn a sanctuary into a prison.

Outside, the world is ablaze, and their village, once vibrant with laughter and life, now lies under the shadow of war. She can feel the weight of it pressing down on her, threatening to suffocate her spirit. "Do you ever think about what you'll do after this is all over?" I ask, my tone softening, as if I am trying to distract her from the present terror. It's a question that lingers at the back of my mind; one I hadn't dare to consider fully. The future feels like a distant dream, a fragile thread that could snap at any moment. "I... I don't know," I admit, my voice trembling. "I want to return to my classroom, to see the children again. But I worry about what will be left of them, of all of us."

Her heart aches at the thought of the innocent faces she has spent years nurturing, now caught in a web of fear and uncertainty. My expression shifts, a flicker of understanding crossing my features. "I can only imagine how hard this is for you. You've dedicated your life to them. It's not just a job; it's your passion." "It is," she replies, her voice thick with emotion. "I wanted to show them the beauty of learning, of the world beyond our village. But now..." Her words falter as the weight of her fears threatens to crush her resolve. I reach out, my hand finding hers, my fingers warm against her cool skin. "You are strong, Elena. You've shown that every day. And when this is all over, you will be there for them. They will need you now more than ever." My grip tightens slightly, as if to anchor her to the moment, to the hope that lies in the future.

She meets my gaze, and for a moment, the chaos outside fades into the background. There's fierce determination in my eyes, a belief that we can overcome this together. It fills her with a flicker of courage, a light that pushes back against the encroaching darkness. "You really think so?" she asks, her voice barely a whisper. "I know so," I reply, my tone unwavering. "You have a fire in you, one that can't be extinguished by this war. And I'll be right there with you, helping to rebuild what's been lost." Elena feels the warmth of my words seep into her bones, igniting a spark of hope that she thought had long been extinguished. "What about you, Jack? What do you want when this is over?" I hesitate, as if searching for the right words. "I want to go home," I finally say, my voice steady but tinged with a longing that resonates deep within me. "But I also want to know that I've made a difference here. That I've fought for something worth fighting for." She watches me as I speak, the passion in my voice igniting a fire within her. "You have. You've given us hope, Jack. Just by being here, you've reminded us that we are not alone." I smile, a genuine expression that lights up my face. "And you, Elena Romano, have given me a reason to fight harder. You've reminded me of what's worth protecting."

Our eyes lock, and in that moment, the fears and uncertainties that plague us seem to fade away. Together, we share a fragile alliance, one built on mutual respect and an understanding of the weight they both carry. The world outside may be crumbling, but within this cave, beneath the Sicilian sky, they find a haven, a shared fear that becomes a source of strength. As the minutes stretch into hours, we sit side by side, our hands entwined, finding comfort in the knowledge that we are not alone in this battle. Outside, the storm rages on, but within the cave, amidst the shadows and flickering light, hope blooms—a fragile flower growing against the odds. And for as long as we are together, we will face whatever comes next, united in our shared fear and the determination to rise above it all.

The air is thick with the scent of damp earth and the distant echoes of artillery, a reminder that the world outside is still engulfed in chaos while we seek refuge within the cool, shadowy embrace of the cave. It feels like a sanctuary, albeit a fragile one, where time itself seems to pause. I sit against the rough wall; my back pressed against the stone and close my eyes to the flickering shadows cast by the dim lantern we've managed to light. Elena is nearby, her silhouette framed by the soft glow. She's tending to the children huddled together on the cave floor, whispering soothing words in Italian, her voice a melodic balm that soothes their frayed nerves. I watch as she moves with a quiet grace, her hands brushing the hair of a small girl who clings to her side. The sight of her—so tender, so strong—stirs something deep within me, a determination that has taken root during our time together. As the rumbling of the distant bombardment reverberates through the cave, I grip my knees tighter, feeling the weight of uncertainty settle heavily on my chest. I need to protect them, to keep this small pocket of life safe from the encroaching darkness.

My thoughts drift to my own squadron, my fellow pilots who are out there, risking everything. I'm torn between two worlds: the duty I owe to my country and the bond I've forged with these people, especially with Elena. She catches my eye, and for a moment, the noise of war fades into the background. Her gaze holds mine, and the connection between us is palpable, a silent understanding that transcends words.

In this moment, I realize that what we've built here is more than mere survival; it's a promise—unspoken yet profound. I vow to protect her, to shield her and the children from the horrors that seem to encroach upon us like a dark tide. "Jack," she whispers, breaking the spell. Her voice is low, almost conspiratorial, as she approaches me, her brow slightly furrowed. "We need to prepare. They might come looking for us."

Her words pull me back to the present, and I nod, pushing away the warmth of my feelings. "You're right. We can't stay here forever." I rise, the urgency of the situation sharpening my focus. I've been a airman long enough to know that complacency can be as dangerous as the enemy. Elena's expression shifts, a flicker of concern crossing her features. "But where will we go? If we leave the cave, we'll be exposed." I take a step closer, my voice low as I try to reassure her. "We need to find a path to safety, a way to get the villagers out of here. There's an old route I saw on the map before I crashed. It leads through the hills. If we can make it, we can reach the next village." Her eyes widen with uncertainty, doubt mingling with the bravery I've come to admire. "Jack, that route is risky. We could run into German patrols. It's dangerous."

I can feel the weight of her fear, the way it coils tightly around her heart, and I want to ease that burden. "I won't let anything happen to you. I promise." The words slip out, a vow that feels as solid as the stone beneath my fingers. I mean it with every fiber of my being. Elena's gaze locks onto mine, searching for the truth in my eyes. "And if something happens to you?" she replies softly, a challenge laced with the vulnerability that makes my heart ache. "What then?" The question hangs in the air, heavy and fraught with the potential of loss. I can't let her think that way. "I won't let that happen either," I assert, my voice firm but gentle. "We'll get through this. Together." Her lips curve into a small, reluctant smile, but it doesn't reach her eyes. The fear still lingers there, and I can't help but reach out, brushing my fingers against her arm, a silent promise that I hope she can feel. The warmth of her skin beneath my touch sends a jolt through me, igniting something deeper than mere affection. It's a bond forged in the fire of adversity, a connection that feels as inevitable as the tides of war.

"Let's gather what we need," I say, breaking the moment but not the spell. "We'll leave at dawn when the light can guide us." She nods, and I see the resolve return to her demeanor. "I'll gather the children's things." As she turns to the group, I can't help but admire her strength. She moves with purpose, her spirit unyielding even in the face of fear. My chest swells with a mix of admiration and protectiveness. I'm not just fighting for the villagers anymore; I'm fighting for her, for this fragile, beautiful thing that has blossomed between us.

The hours pass in a blur as we prepare, the children helping with nervous energy, their innocence a stark contrast to the harsh realities outside. I catch glimpses of Elena as she comforts them, her hands steadying their trembling forms, her laughter cutting through the tension like a ray of sunlight. In those moments, I realize that beneath the Sicilian sky, amidst the chaos of war, I've found something worth fighting for. Not just survival, but a connection that transcends the dark shadows looming over us.

With every shared smile, every whispered promise, we weave a tapestry of hope—a fragile yet unbreakable bond. As the night deepens and the sounds of distant explosions fade into a haunting lullaby, I find myself seated next to her, the cave's cool air wrapping around us like a protective shroud. I want to hold her, to pull her close and shield her from the world, but I settle for a lingering gaze, a silent exchange that speaks volumes. "Whatever happens," I murmur, my voice barely above a whisper, "I'll keep my promise. Elena meets my eyes, and in that moment, everything is clear. The unspoken promise between us isn't just about safety, it's about hope, love, and the unwavering belief that we can emerge from the darkness, together.

9

Unlikely Companions

Beneath a Sky of Hope

The Sicilian sun lingers just above the horizon, a molten disc bleeding amber light across the undulating hills. Shadows stretch long and lean over the parched earth, as though the land itself is exhaling in the fading heat. I narrow my eyes against the brilliance, my pulse quickening as I steal a glance at Elena. Before me, a narrow path winds into the heart of the hills—a trail etched by centuries of passing footsteps, each one is a whisper of stories lost to time. The air is dense with the fragrance of wild thyme, sharp and earthy, and beneath it all, the muted roar of distant waves gnaws steadily at the rocky coast. Yet today, the ancient beauty of this place feels subdued, cloaked in the quiet weight of what lies ahead.

Elena's gaze is steady, her dark eyes reflecting a determination that ignites something deep within me. We have become a team, bound by necessity and forged in the fires of conflict. Together, we have navigated the chaos of war, but now, as we stand on the precipice of the unknown,

Elena can feel the weight of my next step pressing down on her. She takes a deep breath, letting the crisp air fill her lungs, grounding herself in the moment. "Are you ready?" she asks, her voice is low and steady, though she feels anything but. She studies my face, searching for any trace of doubt. Instead, she finds resolve, a fierce light that seems to radiate from her very being. "I was born ready," she replies with a slight smile, her confidence infectious. It's a reminder that she has faced struggles far greater than my own, yet she stands here, unyielding in the face of adversity. She nods, inspired by my spirit. She takes a step forward, and she falls in line beside me. We venture down the path, the rocky surface crunching beneath our boots. Each step feels like a promise to one another, an unspoken vow to protect what we have built together.

As we walk, she reflects on how far we have come. The days of frantic escapes from enemy patrols, the whispered conversations in the dark, the laughter shared over meagre meals, all these moments have woven a tapestry of connection between us. We are no longer just a British pilot and a Sicilian schoolteacher; we are allies, friends, and perhaps something more. The thought sends a shiver through her, both thrilling and terrifying. "Do you think we'll find help?" Elena's question brings her back to the present. She glances up at me; her brow furrowed with concern. "I believe we will," I reply, forcing conviction into her words. "This village has been through so much. They know how to survive. They'll help us." Her lips curl into a soft smile, and she can't help but mirror it. There's beauty in her resilience, a strength that draws me to her. The path ahead is fraught with danger, but with Elena by my side, it feels a little less daunting.

We continue walking in companionable silence, the sound of our footsteps mingling with the rustle of leaves overhead. Her mind races as she considers her next move. There is a need to find a way to communicate with the villagers, to convince them to assist in our plight. The language has been a barrier, but in a shared experience of fear and hope, we have discovered a way to understand one another beyond words. "Maybe we can draw some pictures?" Elena suggests breaking the silence. "I can sketch the plane, and you can explain what we need. Simple images might help convey our message." I chuckle softly, imagining her with a pencil in hand, sketching out their predicament. "I like that idea. You're quite the artist, aren't you?" "Only in moments of inspiration," she replies, her cheeks flushing slightly. "But I think I can manage a simple drawing for survival." I glance at her, admiration swelling in his chest.

"You're incredible, you know that? I don't think I could do this without you." Elena tilts her head, her expression softening. "And I don't think I could do this without you. We make a good team." Our eyes lock for a moment, and I feel a spark of something deeper—an unspoken understanding, a connection that transcends the chaos surrounding us. But before I can ponder it further, they round a bend in the path, revealing a glimpse of the village nestled below. The sight takes my breath away. Sun-drenched rooftops shimmer beneath the azure sky, and the vibrant colours of the market stalls dot the landscape like jewels. Yet, amidst the beauty, a heaviness lingers. The village is quiet, its people wary, shadows of fear etched in our faces as we face the relentless threat of war.

"We need to approach carefully," I advise, my military instincts kicking in. "We don't want to alarm anyone." Elena nods, her expression serious. "Let's find a place where we can observe first. We need to understand what they're dealing with." We make our way to a vantage point, settling behind a cluster of olive trees. From their hiding spot, we watch as villagers go about their daily tasks—some tending to livestock, others gathering what little food they can find. The laughter of children echoes faintly, a reminder of innocence amid the turmoil. "Look," Elena whispers, pointing towards a group of men gathered around a table, their expressions tense as they discuss something in hushed tones. "They seem to be strategizing." I squint, trying to make out their words. "They might be planning how to defend themselves against the German forces. We could offer our assistance." Elena's brow furrows in thought. "But we must be careful. We don't want to put anyone in danger because of us." "Exactly," I agree. "We'll need to approach them slowly, build trust first. They need to know we're not a threat."

As we sit, contemplating our next move, I feel an overwhelming sense of gratitude for this woman beside me. Amid war and uncertainty, Elena has become my anchor, the light guiding me through the darkness. I know that whatever challenges lie ahead, we will face them together. And that thought, more than anything else, fills me with hope. "Let's go," she says finally, determination settling in her bones. "It's time to take that step forward." With that, we rise from our hiding place, hearts pounding in unison. Together, we step into the unknown, ready to face whatever waits beneath the Sicilian sky.

The air is thick with tension and an acrid smell of smoke as she crouches behind the crumbling wall of what once was the village school. The distant roar of aircraft above sends tremors through the earth, and she can feel the reverberations in my chest like a drumbeat of impending doom. Each sound seems magnified—the rustle of leaves, the whispers of the villagers huddled close, even the quickened breaths we both try to stifle. It's a precarious moment, a fragile pause before the storm, and she can't help but glance back.

Her green eyes are fierce yet haunted, a mix of determination and an unspoken fear that binds us together in this moment. I have taken risks that defy reason—flinging me into danger for the sake of others. Today is no different. She can sense that this mission, this need to protect, is more than just duty; it's become personal. "Are you ready?" she asks, her voice low and steady, though she can hear the undercurrent of urgency lacing her words. My heart races at the gravity of her question. It's not just about the mission anymore; it's about trust forged in the fires of chaos, in the heart of war.

I nod, though the truth is I feel as if I am teetering on the edge of an abyss. The villagers have rallied around us, our faces etched with worry, yet there's a strength in our eyes that kindles a flicker of courage within her. She thinks of the children who look to her for reassurance, their small hands clutching at her skirt. They trust her to keep them safe, to be their anchor in this stormy sea of uncertainty.

I catch her gaze, and I can see a question lingering there, unspoken yet palpable. I know she is afraid, perhaps even more than the others. But I also know that I won't back down. I've become a part of this—my mission, our mission—whether I wanted to or not. Each moment we share, each glance exchanged, has built a bridge between us, one that spans the chasm of language and culture.

"Let's go," I say, my voice firm, and I feel that familiar rush of adrenaline surge through me. We creep forward, staying low to the ground, moving like shadows against the backdrop of destruction. With every step, I can feel the weight of the world pressing down on us, but I also feel the warmth of her presence beside me, a beacon of hope amidst the chaos. As we approach the designated meeting point, a dilapidated barn on the outskirts of the village,

I can see the flickering light of lanterns through the cracks in the wooden structure. It serves as a reminder that even in the darkest of nights, there is still a light to guide us home.

The barn is our sanctuary, a place where we can gather our thoughts, share our plans, and, for a moment, breathe. We slip inside, the smell of hay and earth filling my lungs. The villagers have already gathered, our faces a mixture of fear and determination. I step forward, my presence commanding yet gentle. I address them in a mix of English and broken Italian, his words weaving a tapestry of hope and resolve. I stand beside her, feeling the strength of my conviction wash over me. "Tonight, we strike back," I say, my voice steady, a pulse of power that resonates in the hearts of those who listen. "We have a chance to push back against the enemy. To take back what they've stolen from us."

We watch as the villagers nod, their expressions shifting from fear to fierce determination. I look at her, and at that moment, I know that we are in this together. The path ahead is fraught with danger, but we will navigate it side by side. As the plans unfold, I can see the trust between us deepening, each shared glance and nod reinforcing the bond we've formed in this crucible of war. It's a trust that defies the chaos surrounding us, built on the understanding that we are fighting not just for ourselves, but for each other.

When we finish, I turn to her, my eyes searching for her. "Are you ready for this?" I ask, and I can see the concern etched on her face. She takes a deep breath, my heart steadying as she responds, "As ready as I'll ever be. We've come too far to turn back now." She smiles, a fleeting moment of relief washing over her features. "Then let's show them what we're made of."

We step back into the night, the weight of the world still pressing down on us, but now with a shared purpose. The air is electric, charged with the promise of what we might achieve together. She feels the heat of my presence beside her, and she knows that whatever happens, we will face it as one. The path ahead is uncertain, but our trust is an anchor amidst the storm. In this moment, beneath the Sicilian sky, I realize that war may have brought us together, but it is the bond we've forged—an unlikely companionship—that will carry us through the fires of conflict. Together, we will rise and fight, not just for survival, but for love, for hope, and for the future that flickers just beyond the horizon.

The sun hung low in the sky, casting golden rays that filtered through the leaves of the olive trees, creating a mosaic of light and shadow on the ground where Elena and

I sat. We had found a moment of respite amidst the chaos of war, a small clearing on the outskirts of the village where the distant sounds of conflict were muffled, as if the world beyond their sanctuary was merely a whisper. Her laughter rang out, a sound so pure and melodic that it momentarily chased away the haunting spectres of fear that lingered in my mind. She had never imagined that a shared moment could feel so significant, especially in a time when everything seemed uncertain. I watched her as she brushed her stray hair from her face, her hands moving with an elegant grace that belied the harsh reality around them.

The light caught her features, illuminating the determination in her eyes and the softness of her smile. I found myself drawn to her, not just because she was a guiding light in my darkened world, but because of the strength she exuded. It was a strength I admired deeply, a quality that made me want to protect her fiercely even as I felt the weight of my own vulnerabilities. I was an aviator taught to face the enemy with courage, but here, in the presence of this remarkable woman, I felt exposed, as if the armor I wore had been stripped away, leaving me raw and unguarded. "What are you thinking about?" Elena asked, her voice soft, yet laced with curiosity. She caught me staring, her brow arching slightly as she leaned closer, the distance between us shrinking. I hesitated, unsure if I wanted to share the tumult of thoughts swirling in my mind. But there was something about the way she looked at me, those expressive green eyes, brimming with understanding—that urged me to open up. "I was just thinking about how strange it is to find comfort in war," I finally admitted, my voice barely above a whisper. "I've been trained to see enemies, to focus on survival, but with you, it feels different."

Elena nodded, her expression thoughtful. "War forces us to confront what truly matters, doesn't it? It strips away the distractions and lays bare our hearts." She paused, searching for my gaze for something unspoken. "In moments like this, we discover connections we might have never acknowledged otherwise." I felt a heat rising to my cheeks, an unexpected vulnerability flooding through me. "I've never felt so connected to someone in such a short time. It's as if the war around us fades, and all I see is you." Elena's breath hitched, and for a moment, the world outside our bubble ceased to exist. The tension that had been building between us hung in the air, palpable and electric. I could see the way her heart raced, mirroring my own, as if we were two souls intertwining in a dance that transcended the horrors surrounding us.

"Jack…" she started, her voice trembling slightly. "We're in a situation where everything is uncertain, and yet…" Her words trailed off, leaving an invitation hanging between them. "I know," I said, my heart pounding louder than the distant rumble of artillery. "But I can't help but feel drawn to you." Elena shifted closer, the warmth radiating from her body enveloping him. "We're both scared, but maybe that's what makes this connection so powerful. We're not just fighting for survival; we're fighting for the hope of something more." I studied her face, tracing the contours of her features with my gaze. "What if we get through this, and then what? What happens when the war ends? Will we just go back to our separate lives?" "Maybe," I said, a wistful smile gracing her lips. "But I think we'll carry this experience with us, no matter where we end up. We're forever changed."

I feel a lump form in my throat. I wanted to believe her, to embrace that hope with both arms, but fear lingered like a shadow. "I've lost so much already," I confessed. "How do I know I won't lose you too?" Elena reached for my hand, her fingers intertwining with mine, grounding me in that moment. "You won't lose me, Jack. Not if we choose to hold on to what we've found here. We have each other, and that's enough for now." I squeezed her hand, feeling the strength of her resolve in my own. "You're right. I want to cherish this, whatever it is. Just you and me against the world." As the sun slid lower in the sky, painting the horizon in hues of orange and pink, I leaned closer, my heart racing as I searched her eyes for affirmation. Elena mirrored my movement, her breath mingling with mine, creating a shared warmth that seemed to defy the chill of war. In that fleeting moment, the barriers we had erected began to crumble. I could see the flicker of something deeper in her gaze—a longing that mirrored my own. I leaned in, our lips just inches apart, the world around us fading into a distant murmur. Time slowed as if the universe paused to witness their connection, each heartbeat echoing the unspoken promise of what lay ahead.

But before our lips could meet, the sound of distant explosions shattered the tranquility, a harsh reminder of the reality that loomed outside their sanctuary. Elena pulled back, her expression torn between longing and the weight of our circumstances. "Jack, we can't forget—" she began, her voice trembling. "I know," I interrupted gently, brushing my thumb across her knuckles. "But maybe we can hold onto this feeling, this moment, as we navigate the storm ahead."

Elena nodded, her eyes glistening with unshed tears, the gravity of their situation settling heavily upon us. "Together, then," she whispered, sealing the promise with a squeeze of her hands. Together. The word resonated within me, filling the void of uncertainty. I knew the path ahead would be fraught with challenges, but in this moment, beneath the Sicilian sky, I felt a flicker of hope ignite in my heart, fuelled by the strength of our bond—an undeniable connection that had bloomed amidst the chaos of war.

10

The Bond Deepens

Elena stands at the edge of the hillside, A cool breeze stirs the tall grass, brushing softly against her legs and filling the air with the earthy scent of soil mingled with wildflowers. She closes her eyes for a moment, letting the distant chirp of crickets and the gentle rustling of leaves wash over her senses. Drawing a steady breath, Elena feels the weight of uncertainty in her chest but also a spark of quiet determination. As she opens her eyes, she prepares to take the first step toward whatever lies beyond the horizon, her heart both anxious and hopeful in the fading light. The golden hues reflect off the rocky outcrops, illuminating the small village tucked away in the valley below. She takes a deep breath, filling her lungs with the warm, salty air that carries the scent of the Mediterranean. But it is not just the beauty of her surroundings that stirs her; it's the weight of what has been happening around her, the turmoil of war, and the undeniable connection she feels with me.

The thought of us together sends a flutter through her chest. I am the British allied fighter pilot, a man of courage, who is increasingly, playing an important part in her heart. In the days since our paths crossed, she has found herself thinking of me more than she ever thought possible. The way I look at her, with those deep blue eyes that seem to seem to see right into her soul, creates a warmth in her that belies the coldness of the world outside our hidden sanctuary. Elena's thoughts drift back to our first encounter, the panic that had surged through her as she guided the frightened children to safety. She recalls how I had emerged from the smoke, dishevelled yet resolute, and how my presence had instantly grounded her. In those chaotic moments, amidst the fear and uncertainty, I had been her anchor. Now, standing alone, she grapples with the reality of her feelings.

She knows the risks we both face. The war rages on, and each day brings new dangers to their doorstep. Yet, something within her stirs, a resolve to confront her fears, to allow herself to feel. She can no longer deny the hope blooming within her, even as the external world crumbles around them. The villagers depend on her, and she cannot afford to let them down. But how can she support them when she is so drawn to someone who may have to leave at any moment?

As she walks back towards the cave where we have made our refuge, her mind races with thoughts of our shared moments, the quiet conversations, the laughter that breaks through the tension, and the unspoken understanding that flows between us like a current. I have shown her not just resilience but a depth of compassion that she has rarely encountered.

I listen, truly listen, as she shares stories of her students, her family, and her dreams. With each word, he builds a bridge between our worlds, and she feels that bridge becoming a lifeline. In the dim light of the cave, I am seated on a rock, sketching something in the dirt with a stick. When I look up, our eyes meet, and for a moment, time stands still. My face lights up with that signature grin that makes her heart race. "You're back," my voice warm like the sun that has just set outside. "I was beginning to think I'd have to come looking for you." Elena smiles, feeling the tension in her shoulders at ease. "I needed some fresh air to clear my head. It's beautiful out there, but..." "...it's heavy with uncertainty?"

I finish her sentence and look at her to realize her understanding gaze evident on mine. She nods, crossing the small space between them to sit on the ground beside him. "I've never felt such a mix of fear and hope. It's exhausting." I shift slightly, turning to face her more fully. "You've been a beacon of strength for everyone in this village. They need you, Elena. And I can't help but admire how you handle it all." His words fill her with warmth, but they also deepen the weight she carries. "But what about you, Jack? What will happen when this is over? Will you go back to your life, back home, while we remain here, enduring the aftermath of this war? He looks down, his expression clouding for a moment. "I don't know," he admits, his voice low. "My duty calls, but..." I hesitate, searching for the right words. "This place, you—what we've built here—it's not something I can just walk away from." Elena's heart skips a beat. She feels the intensity of the moment, the gravity of our connection pressing down on her. "But it's not just you and me, Jack. There's so much at stake. We're living in a war zone. How can we think about anything else?" "Because we have to," I reply, his eyes locking onto hers with an intensity that sends shivers down her spine. "In the midst of chaos, we find our humanity. We must hold on to hope, to the possibility of something more." My words resonate deeply within her, igniting a flame of determination. "You're right. I can't let fear dictate my actions. I've spent too long worrying about what might happen instead of living in the moment. We're here now, and we can make a difference—together."

I lean closer, a spark of excitement lighting my features. "Together," he echoes, and the promise of that word hangs in the air, heavy with unspoken possibilities. Elena feels a surge of confidence. She knows this is her moment to embrace her resolve. "I want to help you, Jack. I want to be part of this fight—not just for my village but for us, for everything we can stand for together." A soft smile breaks over my face, and she can see the admiration in my eyes. "Then we'll do it. We'll plan, we'll fight, and we'll protect each other. I won't let you face this alone." In that moment, Elena knows that no matter what lies ahead, she has made her choice. She will stand with me, against the odds, against the war, and against the fear that has threatened to consume her. Together, we will forge a new path beneath the Sicilian sky, a path illuminated by the strength of our bond and the resilience of our hearts.

The sun hangs high in the Sicilian sky, casting a golden hue over the village nestled among the undulating hills. The distant echoes of war feel muted today, as if the world has paused just for a moment, allowing us to breathe deeply and savour the fragile peace. I stand at the entrance of our makeshift shelter—a cave that has become a second home—watching Elena as she tends to the small garden that has sprung up like a miracle among the craggy rocks. Her hands are skilled and gentle, coaxing life from the earth. I can't help but admire her focus, the way she bends low to inspect the delicate green shoots that promise sustenance. Each leaf seems to absorb the warmth of her spirit, thriving under her care. It's a stark contrast to the harsh reality just beyond the village's borders, where the rumble of artillery and the cries of the frightened linger like a dark cloud.

I carefully step into the sunlight, the warmth enveloping me like a comforting embrace. "Need any help?" I call out, my voice tinged with a casualness I don't entirely feel. Elena looks up, her brown eyes sparkling as they meet mine. "I could always use another set of hands," she replies with a bright smile that instantly fills the air with warmth. It's infectious, and I feel a smile tugging at my own lips as I walk over to join her. As I kneel beside her, the scent of soil and wildflowers fills my senses, grounding me in the moment. "What are we planting today?" I ask, curious about her little hidden oasis amid the chaos. "Tomatoes and basil," she explains, her fingers deftly working the soil. "They can grow well together and make a lovely sauce." She pauses, glancing at me with a hint of mischief. "If we can find some pasta, that is."

The thought of a simple meal shared, however improbable, ignites a warmth in my chest. "I'll do my best to find some," I promise, imagining how wonderful it would be to sit around a table, savouring a meal that tastes of home, even if it's just for a fleeting moment. As we work side by side, the conversation flows easily between us, weaving a tapestry of shared experiences and dreams for the future.

I learn more about her life before the war, her childhood spent running through the sun-drenched fields, the laughter of her students echoing in her classroom, the way she used to dream of traveling beyond Sicily's shores. "I always wanted to see the world," she admits, a wistful look crossing her face. "But now... now I just want to keep my village safe." Her words strike a chord deep within me. I know all too well the sacrifices made in the name of duty and loyalty. "You're doing that, you know," I say softly, meeting her gaze. "You're protecting them. You're a beacon of hope." Elena blushes slightly, brushing a stray strand of hair behind her ear. "I don't feel like a beacon. I'm just doing what I can." Her humility is endearing, yet I see the strength that drives her, the determination that fuels her actions.

"Sometimes, that's all it takes," I reply, emboldened by the bond we've forged in the face of adversity. There's a connection between us that transcends language, built on shared fears and aspirations. We share a quiet moment, the only sounds being the gentle rustle of leaves and the distant chirping of birds. It feels like a dream, a slice of normalcy amidst the chaos of war. I reach over, brushing my fingertips against her hand, and she looks up, her eyes wide with surprise. "Jack..." she begins, but I squeeze her hand gently, needing her to understand the depth of my feelings without the need for words. "I know we're in the middle of something that seems insurmountable," I say, my voice steady. "But this moment—this calm—reminds me of what we're fighting for." Her expression softens, and for a heartbeat, the tension that has lingered between us dissipates. "I wish I could believe that," she whispers, her voice barely audible.

"Believe it," I urge, my heart racing as I lean closer. "We have to believe that one day, the sun will rise again without the shadow of war hanging over us." Elena nods slowly, and the uncertainty in her eyes melts away, replaced by a flicker of hope. "You make it sound possible," she replies, a hint of a smile returning to her lips. We continue to plant the seeds in silent companionship, the rhythm of our movements synchronizing in a dance of unspoken understanding. Each seed represents a dream, a hope for a future untainted by violence, and I find solace in the idea that we're nurturing not just a garden, but the very essence of life itself.

As the sun begins its descent, painting the sky in shades of orange and pink, I take a moment to appreciate the beauty surrounding us. The village feels alive, vibrant with possibility. Laughter echoes from nearby children, their carefree spirits, a stark reminder of what we stand to protect. "Do you think we'll ever see a day when this is just a memory?" I venture, the question hanging in the air between us. "Yes," Elena replies with conviction, her gaze fixed on the horizon where the sun meets the earth. "I believe we will. And when that day comes, we'll share a meal together, just like we imagined." Her words wrap around me like a promise, and I can't help but smile at the thought of that future. "Then it's a date," I say, trying to lighten the weight of reality. "Just don't forget the pasta," she teases, and the laughter that spills from her lips is like music, lifting the burden of angst that has clung to us for too long.

As we finish our work, the last rays of sunlight dance across the landscape, illuminating the world beneath the Sicilian sky. In this moment, amidst the uncertainty and fear, I find a flicker of hope—our bond deepening, rooted in resilience and love. The sun hangs low in the Sicilian sky, casting a golden hue across the hills, as if the heavens themselves are conspiring to create a moment of beauty amidst the chaos that surrounds us. The air is thick with the scent of wildflowers and the distant tang of salt from the sea. I find myself sitting on the edge of a weathered stone wall, my heart racing not from the fear of war, but from something far more bewildering—Elena. She approaches me, her silhouette framed by the shimmering light, and for a moment, the world falls away. The sounds of distant gunfire and the murmurs of the villagers fade into a soft hum, replaced by the rhythm of my own heartbeat. As she draws closer, I can see the determination in her eyes mingling with a flicker of uncertainty. We are two souls caught in a tempest, and yet, in this fleeting moment, we are also the calm. "Jack," she says, her voice a soft whisper that dances through the air, brushing against my skin like a gentle breeze.

"There's something I need to show you." The urgency in her tone pulls me from my thoughts, and I nod, my curiosity piqued. She leads me through the narrow streets of the village, our footsteps echoing against the cobblestones, and I'm acutely aware of the warmth radiating from her hand as it brushes against mine. It's a connection that feels electric, a thread weaving us closer together. I glance at her, and for a heartbeat, I see the walls she has built around herself begin to crack. We arrive at a small clearing, surrounded by ancient olive trees that seem to bow under the weight of history. The sun filters through the leaves, casting playful shadows on the ground. It's an enchanting sanctuary, untouched by the horrors of the outside world. Elena steps into the sunlight, her face illuminated, and I can't help but marvel at her beauty, at the way she embodies both strength and vulnerability.

"Here," she says, motioning for me to follow her deeper into the grove. The air is cooler here, filled with the rustling of leaves and the distant call of birds. She stops at a gnarled tree, its trunk twisted and knotted yet standing resolute against the winds of time. "This tree has seen so much," she continues, her voice barely above a whisper. "It's survived storms, droughts, and now, war. Just like us."

I take a step closer, the weight of her words settling heavily in the air between us. "It's beautiful," I reply, feeling a surge of admiration not just for the tree, but for the woman standing beside it. She looks at me, her eyes brightening as if she's searching for something in my gaze. "Do you believe we can survive this?" she asks, vulnerability creeping into her tone. "That we can emerge on the other side, no matter how battered?" In that moment, I realize that our hearts are dancing the same rhythm, caught in a waltz of hope and despair. I reach out, capturing her gaze and holding it steady. "I have to believe we can," I say, my voice steady despite the tremor in my chest. "Because if we don't, then what's left for us?" Elena steps closer, the space between us evaporating. "You're right," she breathes, and I can see the resolve hardening in her expression. "We have to hold on to something—anything—worth fighting for."

Her words strike a chord within me, resonating against the tumult within. I take a breath, the air thick with possibilities. Leaning in, I can feel the warmth radiating from her skin, and for a moment, the weight of the world slips away. In this haven, beneath the old olive tree, we find solace in each other's presence. "Then let's fight," I say, my voice low but fervent. "Together." Her lips curve into a soft smile, and my heart quickens at the sight. It's a smile that feels like a promise, a tether that binds us in this moment.

The air hums with unspoken words, and I can no longer resist the pull between us. I reach out, brushing a stray hair from her face, and the contact sends a jolt through me—one that ignites something deep within. "Jack…" she murmurs, her voice trembling as she looks up at me, her eyes wide and trusting. I lean closer, my breath mingling with hers, and as our lips meet, time stands still. It's a tentative kiss at first, a whisper of what is to come, but as she responds, deepening the connection, it becomes a declaration—a promise of what lies ahead. The world around us fades into oblivion, and all that exists is the warmth of our bodies, the beating of our hearts, and the intoxicating scent of her hair. In that moment, beneath the Sicilian sky, we are no longer just Jack and Elena. We are two souls entwined, dancing to a melody only we can hear—a dance that transcends the horrors of war, a dance that speaks of hope, love, and a future worth fighting for. As we part, breathless, I feel a renewed sense of purpose. Whatever challenges lie ahead, I know we will face them together, our bond forged in the fires of adversity. And as I look into her eyes, I see the glimmer of hope shining brighter than ever—a beacon guiding us through the darkness, beneath the Sicilian sky.

11

Echoes Of Conflict

The air crackles with tension, thick with the scent of smoke and the distant rumble of artillery. I stand at the edge of the cave, peering out into the dimming light of dusk. My heart pounds as I wonder if tonight will bring relief or more chaos, the uncertainty gnawing at me with every echo from the battlefield. The sun hangs low on the horizon, casting a bloody hue over the hills of Sicily. It's beautiful and horrific all at once. I can hear Elena's soft voice from behind me, soothing the frightened children huddled together, their wide eyes reflecting the fear that has become a near-constant companion in these dark times. I glance back at her, and for a fleeting moment, the chaos outside fades. She's kneeling beside a small boy, brushing dirt from his cheek, whispering words of comfort. There's something so fragile about the scene, the way she fights to maintain a semblance of normalcy amidst the horror surrounding us. But as I look into her eyes, I see the shadows creeping in.

The weight of the war presses down on her, and I feel it too, a shared burden that neither of us can escape. "Elena," I call softly, my voice barely above a whisper. She looks up, her gaze locking onto mine. The brief connection sends a jolt through me, a reminder that in this world of turmoil, we still have each other. "Jack," she replies, straightening up. There's a quiver in her voice, and I know she's trying to mask her fear. "I think they're getting closer."

I nod, my heart sinking at the thought. The German forces are tightening their grip on the region, and each day, the sounds of conflict grow nearer. It's a constant reminder that we are living on borrowed time, hidden away in this cave, a fragile sanctuary amid the storm. I step closer to her, the weight of my uniform heavy around my shoulders. "We need to be ready," I say, my voice low and steady. "If they come here..."

She bites her lip, her eyes flickering with uncertainty. "What do we do, Jack? They'll find us. They always find us." I can see the flicker of doubt in her eyes, and it gnaws at me. I wish I could promise her that everything will be alright, that we'll find a way out of this hell, but the truth is, I don't know. The world outside is chaotic, and the shadows of conflict loom larger each day. "Listen," I say, taking her hands in mine, feeling the warmth of her skin against the coolness of the cave. "We'll find a way to keep them safe. You've done so much already for these kids. You're stronger than you think." Her gaze drops, and I can see the struggle within her. "What if it's not enough? What if we can't protect them?" I squeeze her hands tighter, willing her to see what I see. "We can't let fear win. We have to trust that there's still hope. We must believe that something good can come from this."

Elena's eyes meet mine again, and for a moment, the world outside fades away. There's a connection between us, a silent understanding that transcends the chaos. But just as quickly as I feel that bond, the sound of distant gunfire shatters the moment, a stark reminder of our reality. Her expression darkens, and I can see it—the shadow of despair creeping into her heart. "Jack, what if—" I cut her off, my voice urgent. "No. We can't think like that. We must focus on what we can control. We must prepare." A group of children gathers around her, their faces pale and drawn. She kneels, pulling them close, her voice gentle as she speaks to them. I watch her, captivated by the way she becomes their anchor, a beacon of light in the darkness. In this moment, she embodies everything I admire about her, her strength, her courage, her unwavering resolve to protect those she loves. But the shadows don't recede. Instead, they deepen, wrapping around us like a suffocating blanket. I can feel the weight of the impending threat pressing down, an ominous feeling that something is coming—something we can't escape.

As the night settles in, I stand guard at the cave entrance, my heart pounding in rhythm with the distant sounds of war. The moon casts a silvery glow over the hills, illuminating the chaos that lies just beyond our sanctuary. I scan the horizon, my instincts heightened, every sound amplified in the stillness. "Elena," I call over my shoulder, my voice steady. "Stay close to the children. Keep them quiet." She nods, her expression resolute, but I can see the flicker of fear behind her eyes. The shadows of conflict are closing in, and I know that soon, we may have to face the enemy together. I steel myself for what's to come, the tension in my muscles coiling like a spring. There's a storm brewing, and I can't shake the feeling that it's only a matter of time before it breaks.

The night grows colder, the air heavy with anticipation. I take a deep breath, trying to push away the encroaching dread. I can't let myself falter—not now, not when Elena and the children are counting on me. I've fought battles in the sky, where the enemy was faceless and distant. But this battle is different. It's personal, and the stakes are higher than I've ever known. As the echoes of conflict grow closer, I vow to protect Elena, to keep her and the children safe. The shadows may loom large, but I refuse to let them consume us. Together, we will stand against the darkness, our hearts entwined beneath the Sicilian sky. The sun dips low on the horizon, casting long shadows across the village, a harbinger of the dusk that blankets Sicily in a warm, golden hue. I stand at the mouth of the cave, the air thick with the scent of damp earth and fading smoke from the last shelling.

My heart races, not just from the proximity of danger, but from the weight of the decision looming before me. The war is calling, and I am torn between duty and a bond that has consumed my thoughts since I first laid eyes on Elena. The villagers, weary and worn, gather around the small fire they've managed to light, their faces flickering in the orange glow. They sense the change in the air, too. The fear is palpable, but there is also an undercurrent of hope, hope that rests on the shoulders of a stranger who has become part of their world. I can't let them down. And yet, I can't shake the image of Elena's face as I prepare to leave. Her eyes glisten with unshed tears, a reflection of everything we have come to mean to each other amidst the chaos.

"Jack," she calls softly, stepping closer, her silhouette framed against the fading light. The softness of her voice pulls at my heart, and I turn to face her. "You don't have to do this. We can find another way. We can stay here, together." The desperation in her plea stings. I want nothing more than to stay, to bask in the warmth of her presence, to shield her from the horrors that lurk beyond the hills. But I know the truth.

My fellow pilots are counting on me, and the mission is critical. The Allies are pushing deeper into enemy territory, and every soldier, every pilot, counts in this fight. "Elena," I call to her, my voice steady despite the turmoil inside. "I must go back. They need me. We can't let the Germans hold this village. If I can help turn the tide, if I can buy you all sometime…" She closes the distance between us, her gaze fierce yet tender. "And what about us? What if you don't come back? What then?" The question hangs in the air, heavy and unyielding. I reach out, brushing a strand of hair behind her ear. It's a simple gesture, but it carries all the weight of my affection, my promise to return. "I will come back, Elena. I promise you that. This isn't the end for us. It's just a pause… a moment in time."

Her breath catches, and for a moment, the world around us fades. It's just her and me, beneath the Sicilian sky, where hope and despair intertwine. I see the resolve in her eyes, but also the flicker of fear. "Just be careful, Jack. The war doesn't play fair." I nod, swallowing hard against the lump in my throat. "I will be careful. I promise. But I need you to believe in me, to believe that I'll return." With a trembling hand, she reaches up and cups my cheek, her touch like fire against my skin. "I believe in you, Jack. Just… don't let this war take you from me."

I lean into her palm, feeling the warmth radiate through me. "I won't. Not if I can help it." The moment stretches, and I wish I could freeze time, hold onto this feeling forever. But the distant rumble of artillery reminds me that time waits for no one. With a heavy heart, I pull away and turn to face the villagers gathered around the fire. They look at me with a mix of hope and fear, and I realize I owe them more than just a promise to return. I owe them my courage, my strength.

"We're going to need every able hand," I say, my voice carrying across the flickering flames. "We have to prepare for what's coming. I'll go back and do my part, but you all must be ready to defend what's ours." Murmurs of agreement ripple through the group, and I can see their spirits rising, fuelled by a shared purpose. It's a small victory, but it's enough. As the night deepens, I gather what little supplies I have left, a few rations, a map, my sidearm. Each item feels like a weight added to my resolve, and yet, I can't shake the feeling that I'm leaving a piece of myself behind. I look back one last time at Elena, standing by the cave's entrance, her silhouette, a beacon of strength and grace. "Stay safe, Jack," she whispers, her voice barely audible over the wind.

With a final nod, I step away from the cave, my heart pounding with every step I take into the unknown. The village fades behind me, replaced by the rugged terrain of the Sicilian hills. The shadows stretch, but I push forward, driven by the promise of returning to her, to the life we could build together if I survive this. The night is alive with the sounds of war, the distant thud of artillery and the whisper of the wind through the trees. I carry Elena's words with me, each syllable a reminder of what I'm fighting for. As I navigate the treacherous paths back to the front lines, I feel the weight of my duty pressing down on me, but it's tempered by the knowledge that love can flourish even in the darkest of times.

I will return; I tell myself. For her. For us. Beneath the Sicilian sky. The sun sinks low in the Sicilian sky, casting long shadows across the village, where the remnants of laughter and life coexist with the weight of uncertainty. I stand at the edge of the cave, the cool stone pressing against his back, grounding him in this moment.

The air is thick with tension, a feeling that has become all too familiar. He glances toward the heart of the village, where the sounds of children playing and women chatting mingle with the distant rumble of artillery. It's a stark contrast to the turmoil in his chest. Elena appears from the path leading down from the village, her silhouette framed by the fading light. She walks with purpose yet carries an air of fragility that makes him ache. The dark curls of her hair dance in the evening breeze, and as she approaches, the softness of her expression brings him momentary peace. Perhaps it is the way she focuses on him, her eyes searching his, as if seeking reassurance amid the chaos that surrounds them. "Jack," she says, breathless, as she reaches him. Her voice is a melody he never tires of hearing. "We need to talk." I nod, though my heart sinks. We both know what this conversation entails. The truth hangs heavy between us, and neither of us can ignore it any longer.

I take a step closer, wanting to bridge the distance that seems to grow with every passing day. "I know," he replies, his voice steady despite the turmoil beneath. "It's about the mission." Elena's brow furrows slightly as she processes his words. "You can't go, Jack. You know that. It's too dangerous." There's a tremor in her voice, a mixture of fear and fierce determination that tugs at him. "I have to," I insist, the weight of duty pressing down on me. "I can't just sit here while this war rages on. People are suffering, and I can help. I must try." "But what about us?" she breathes, her eyes glistening with unshed tears. They both know that the war has already taken so much from us. The bond they forged in the heat of chaos feels both fragile and vital, yet the looming specter of uncertainty threatens to shatter it. "What if you don't come back?"

I reach for her, cupping her face in my hands, feeling the warmth of her skin against my palms. "Elena, listen to me. You've shown me what it means to fight for something worth saving. I can't abandon that—abandon you." Her breath hitches, and I can see the battle waging inside her. The strength that defines her falters, and for a moment, she looks so vulnerable, so beautifully human. "And what about your life? Your dreams? Do they mean nothing?" "Everything I've seen in this war has made me realize what truly matters," I reply, his heart racing as he searches her gaze for understanding. "It's not just about flying missions. It's about fighting for people like you—people who inspire hope even when all seems lost." Elena's resolve softens, but she shakes her head, her voice steadier now, though still edged with sorrow. "You're asking me to accept losing you, Jack. I don't know if I can. You're not just a air captain to me. You're... everything."

My heart twists painfully at my words, and I wonder if she can see just how deeply she has rooted herself in his soul. "You're everything to me too," I confess, the truth pouring out like a lifeline. "But I can't turn my back on this fight. I need you to believe in me, in what I'm doing. I promise—I'll do everything I can to come back to you." The silence that follows is heavy; a chasm filled with unspoken fears and desperate hopes. My fingers linger on her skin, my heart pounding as I search for the right words to bridge the gap between us. "I don't want to leave you like this," I murmur, the weight of my decision pressing down on me like a leaden shroud.

Elena's eyes lock onto mine, and I see the flicker of determination return. "Then don't," she replies, her strength resurfacing like the dawn breaking after a long night. "Stay here with me. We can find a way through this together." I want to believe her, to lay down my arms and surrender to the peace that her presence brings. But I know the reality of war, the urgency of the mission that calls to me like a siren song. "I can't. I wish I could, but I have to go. For the village, for you."

A soft sob escapes her lips, and my heart shatters as I watch tears spill down my cheek. I pull her into an embrace, burying my face in her hair, inhaling the scent of her—lavender and hope intertwined. "I promise I'll come back," he whispers fervently, as if his words could rewrite fate. "I'll fight for you, for us. Just hold on to that." She clings to me tightly, and in that moment, they are two souls intertwined beneath the Sicilian sky, fighting against the shadows that threaten to engulf us. Time stretches, and for a fleeting moment, the world around them falls away, leaving only the echo of their hearts beating in sync. Eventually, Elena pulls back, her expression shifting from despair to resolve. "Then I will wait for you, Jack. No matter how long it takes." Her voice is steady, filled with a fierce determination that makes him want to fight harder, to survive against all odds.

"Promise me you'll stay safe," I urge, my grip tightening around her hands. "Promise me you won't let the darkness take you." "I promise," she replies, her gaze unwavering. "You're not the only one fighting here. I'll do everything I can to protect this village, to protect our home. And I'll keep the hope alive for you." With those words, we share a lingering kiss, a blend of desperation and love that seals our promises. I know I must leave, but as I step back, I feel as if a part of me remains with her, tethered by a bond that transcends time and war. As I turn away, the ache in my chest deepens, but I carry her strength with me, a flicker of light in the darkness. Our paths may diverge, but beneath the Sicilian sky, our souls are forever intertwined, echoing the love that will guide us home.

Elena stands at the edge of the hillside, the sun dipping low in the sky, casting long shadows across the landscape. The golden hues reflect off the rocky outcrops, illuminating the small village tucked away in the valley below. She takes a deep breath, filling her lungs with the warm, salty air that carries the scent of the Mediterranean. But it is not just the beauty of her surroundings that stirs her; it's the weight of what has been happening around her, the turmoil of war, and the undeniable connection she feels for me.

12

The War Within

Elena purposely sits on the edge of the bed in the small room she has claimed as her own within the village's refuge, I can see her fingers are absentmindedly tracing the faded pattern of the worn quilt. The faint scent of lavender mingles with the mustiness of old stone, and muted voices drift through the thin walls, reminding her both of the fragile safety and crowded uncertainty that surround her. A single shaft of late afternoon light slants through the narrow window, catching dust motes that dance in the stillness. Elena's shoulders are tight with anxiety, her heart heavy as she tries to steady her breath—each moment alone amplifying her worry about what tomorrow might bring, and the ache of missing those she loves. The air is heavy with the scent of damp earth and the faint whiff of smoke from the fires that burn outside, remnants of a battle that refuses to relent. Wrapping her arms around herself, Lena feels a chill that has nothing to do with the weather—she is uncertain whether the walls shelter her from the chaos or simply remind her of what she has lost. Each distant explosion and echo of rifle fire serves as a stark reminder of how war has altered the rhythm of life here, leaving the village scared and its people, including Lena, clinging to any sense of normalcy amidst the upheaval. The refuge offers her a fragile sanctuary, yet the relentless sounds and smells of conflict seep in, blurring the line between safety and sorrow.

She stares at the cracked wall, tracing the jagged lines with her finger, as though they could tell her a story of hope rather than despair. The world outside is a war zone, and yet, within her, the most tumultuous battle rages on, a war of the heart. My absence feels like a void, one that expands with each passing hour. She had grown accustomed to my presence, my laughter ringing in the air like a melody, my fierce determination igniting a spark in her own spirit. But now, it is quiet. The echoes of our shared moments linger in the corners of her mind, reminding her of the connection we forged amidst the chaos. Each memory is a bittersweet reminder of what she has come to cherish, the warmth of my hand brushing against hers, the way her eyes light up when I speak of my dreams of home, and the moments of silence that speak louder than words.

She closes her eyes, allowing herself to be enveloped by the memories. The first time we had met, I had stumbled into her life like a whirlwind, my British bravado contrasting sharply with her cautious nature. The language barrier had felt insurmountable at first, but as we shared smiles and gestures, she found herself drawn to me in a way she had never expected. My laughter was a balm against the harsh reality of war, and my presence filled her with an uncanny sense of safety, even when danger lurked just outside our sanctuary.

But now, with me away on a mission—that could change the tide of the war—her heart aches with uncertainty. She had watched me leave, a mixture of pride and fear swelling within her. I had turned to her, my expression serious yet tender, as he promised to return. "I'll come back for you, Elena. I swear it," I had said, my voice steady, but she could see the flicker of doubt behind my bravado. In that moment, she wanted to believe me, to hold onto the hope that I would return and that we could build a life together beyond the confines of this war-torn village. Yet, the weight of reality presses down on her. News travels slowly in these hills, but whispers of battles fought, and lives lost reach her ears like a relentless tide. She cannot shake the feeling of dread that coils around her heart, squeezing tighter with each day that passes.

What if I do not come back? What if this is the last time she sees me? The thought is unbearable, gnawing at her insides like a hungry beast. Elena rises from the bed, pacing the small room, the wooden floor creaking under her weight. She needs to do something. She cannot just sit and wait for news that may never come. The villagers depend on her, and she has a responsibility to them, to the children who look to her for guidance and comfort. She can't let her fear consume her, even as it threatens to swallow her whole.

Stepping outside, the cool evening breeze greets her, rustling the leaves of the olive trees that dot the landscape. She inhales deeply, filling her lungs with the scent of the earth, the promise of rain lingering in the air. The village is quiet, but the tension is palpable. She can sense it in the way the villagers move about—cautiously, eyes darting to the horizon, waiting for the sound of approaching planes or the rumble of distant artillery.

As she makes her way to the makeshift schoolhouse, her heart aches with longing. The children are her refuge, their laughter a soothing balm for her troubled soul. They greet her with wide smiles, their innocence a stark contrast to the horrors that surround them. She kneels down, enveloping a small girl in her arms, the child's giggles breaking through the fog of her heartache. "Miss Elena!" the girl exclaims, her eyes sparkling with joy. "Will we have story time today?" Elena nods, her own smile faltering slightly as she gathers the children around her. She opens the tattered book filled with tales of adventure and heroism, each word a reminder of the bravery that exists even in the darkest of times.

As she reads aloud, she watches their faces illuminate with imagination, their worries momentarily forgotten. But as the stories unfold, her thoughts drift back to the time we met. She wonders if I am reading stories to a squadron of soldiers or airmen, or if I am thinking of her amidst the chaos. The ache in her heart intensifies, a deep yearning for the man who has unknowingly captured her soul. The children's laughter rings in her ears, but it is my laughter that she longs to hear, my voice a melody she can't quite forget. The sun begins to set, casting a warm golden hue over the village. She watches as the children run off to their homes, their spirits lifted, but her heart remains heavy. As she stands alone, the weight of the world seems to settle on her shoulders. She feels lost in this moment, a solitary figure against the backdrop of a war that refuses to relent. With a deep breath, she closes her eyes and allows the tears to fall. She doesn't care if anyone sees her; in this moment of vulnerability, she is simply a woman overwhelmed by love and fear.

She whispers a silent prayer to the universe, begging for my safety, for their love to endure the trials of war. And beneath the Sicilian sky, she finds solace in the stars beginning to twinkle above her, each one a reminder that even in the darkest times, light can still pierce through the shadows. She holds onto that thought as she returns to the refuge, her heart aching yet hopeful, knowing that whatever may come, her love for me will always remain a beacon guiding her through the storm. The echo of distant gunfire reverberates through the valley, a grim reminder of the war that encircles us like a relentless storm. Sitting on the edge of the cave, I find my thoughts consumed by the chaos outside and the turmoil within. The flickering light of the small fire casts shadows on the rocky walls, dancing in rhythm with the uncertainty that gnaws at my heart. She thinks of the English pilot who has become such an integral part of her life and wonders what I am feeling.

The weight of the world rests heavily on her shoulders. The village she has devoted herself to is at the mercy of the enemy, she can only do so much to protect them. She is a teacher by trade, not a warrior. Yet, here she is, thrust into a battle that stretches far beyond the physical conflict. She feels torn between her duty to her people and the growing bond she shares with me. It's a war of the heart, one that is just as fierce as the one raging outside. Every day has become a delicate dance of survival. She finds solace in the brief moments when she steals away from the chaos shared glance, a quiet conversation in the dim light of the cave, or the gentle brush of her hands as they pass supplies. But with each fleeting moment, she is reminded of the reality that this may not last. The thought of losing me sends a shiver down her spine, awakening fear I never thought I could harbour. What if she could allow herself to love me fully, only to have the war claim her, too? The weight of that possibility suffocates her, yet the emotions she feels for me are impossible to ignore.

I have become her anchor in these turbulent seas, a beacon of hope against the backdrop of despair. But hope is a dangerous thing, fragile, easily shattered. She closes her eyes, recalling every moment we've shared. The way she listened intently as I speak, my blue eyes filled with understanding. The warmth of my smile that ignites something deep within me, something that feels both exhilarating and terrifying. She can't deny the connection we share, but she is haunted by the knowledge that our time together is fleeting. As the night deepens, the sounds of war faded into a distant murmur, and she felt a pull toward the heart of her conflict. She must choose between the safety of her heart and the risk of love. She stood and walked to the mouth of the cave, gazing out at the stars that peppered the Sicilian sky.

They twinkle like the dreams she once had, dreams of a peaceful life, of laughter filling the schoolroom, of children growing up free from the shadows of war. But the dreams feel distant now, overshadowed by the harsh reality of survival. She cannot allow herself to dwell on what could have been. Instead, she should focus on the present, on the people who rely on her. The village, the children, they are her responsibility. She cannot abandon them, nor can I. My heart is caught in a tempest, torn between two worlds. A soft footfall behind her breaks her reverie. She turns to find me, my silhouette framed by the moonlight, a warrior and yet so much more. I step closer, my face shadowed but my eyes bright with something I dare to hope is love. "Elena," I say, my voice low and steady, "What's on your mind?" she takes a breath, feeling the weight of her emotions swell within her. "I'm afraid," she confesses, the words spilling from her lips before she can stop them. "Afraid for my village, for the children, and… for us." The vulnerability in her voice hangs between us, and for a moment, the world outside fades away.

I step closer, bridging the distance that the war has created. "We are fighting for them," I reply, my hand reaching out to cradle her cheek. "And for us. We have to believe that there is something worth fighting for, something that can survive this madness." My touch sends a jolt through her, igniting a flicker of hope that she desperately clings to. "But what if this ends in loss?" She whispers, her voice barely above breath. "What if this love is another casualty of war?"

My gaze deepens; my expression is a mix of determination and tenderness. "Elena, love is never a casualty. It's what keeps us alive. It's the reason we fight. If we don't hold onto it, we lose ourselves in the darkness." My words resonate within her, and she feels the walls she has constructed around her heart begin to crumble. The war may take many things from us, but it cannot take away the love we choose to nurture. "But how do we protect it?" she asks, her voice trembling with the weight of her fears.

"We protect it by living it," I reply, my thumb tracing her jawline, sending shivers down her spine. "We fight for it, every single day. We make sacrifices, but we never let fear dictate our choices." Tears well in her eyes, blurring the starlit sky. I realize that I have let fear cloud my judgment for too long. My presence reminds her that love is worth every risk, every heartache. It is the one thing that can transcend the chaos of war and bind us together, even in the darkest hours. As she leans into my touch, she feels a sense of clarity wash over her. She chooses to embrace our love, to fight for it with every fibre of her being. She will not allow the war to dictate the terms of her heart. She will stand strong, not just for her village, but for myself and the connection we share. In that moment, beneath the vast Sicilian sky, I make a silent promise to myself: I will love fiercely, even amidst the turmoil. I will fight for the hope that blooms in the face of despair. Because in this world ravaged by war, love is the one thing worth believing in.

The air hangs thick with the scent of smoke and despair. I stand at the edge of the village, peering into the distance where the mountains rise like sentinels against the bruised sky. The sun, a feeble orb, struggles to break through the heavy clouds that blanket us, casting a muted light over the remnants of what was once a vibrant community. Today, however, the laughter of children is replaced by the haunting echoes of loss, and the lively chatter of villagers has given way to a tense silence, punctuated only by the distant rumble of artillery. I can't shake the feeling that I'm losing Elena. Each day, as the war inches closer, the distance between us seems to grow. She carries the weight of her people's suffering on her shoulders, a burden that threatens to crush her spirit. I watch her from afar, her figure silhouetted against the backdrop of the crumbling village, and it pains me to see the light in her eyes dimming. She's always been a beacon of strength, but now, the flicker of hope that once burned so brightly within her is waning.

My heart clenches as I recall the warmth of her smile, the way she would laugh, even in the face of danger. She cared for the children with gentle hands and a soothing voice, revealing the woman I came to love. Yet, the war's horrors persist, threatening to tear us apart. As I walk through the village, I find myself drawn to the small schoolhouse where Elena teaches. The building is battered, its windows shattered, yet it stands resilient, much like its inhabitants. I push open the door, the creak echoing in the stillness, and step inside. Dust motes dance in the shafts of light that filter through the cracks, illuminating the remnants of what was once a sanctuary of learning. Desks sit empty, their surfaces marred by scratches and scars of neglect, and I can almost hear the echoes of laughter that once filled this space.

"Jack." Elena's voice cuts through the silence, pulling me from my reverie. She stands in the doorway, her eyes wide with surprise, then softening into something warmer. There's a moment of stillness as we take each other in, the world outside fading away. The lines of worry etched on her face seem to soften in my presence, if only for a moment. "Hey," I reply, forcing a smile that doesn't quite reach my eyes. "I wanted to see you."

Her gaze flickers to the empty classroom, the reality of our circumstances creeping back in. "It's not safe here, Jack. You shouldn't be—" "I need to be here," I interrupt gently, stepping closer. "I can't just stand by while everything falls apart. I care about you. About all of this." I wave my hand around the room, encompassing the village, the children, the dreams that hang like fragile threads in the air. Elena's expression softens, and I see a flicker of that fierce spirit I admire so much. "I don't want to put you in danger," she says, her voice trembling slightly. "Things are getting worse. The Germans are tightening their grip. We've lost so many already."

"I know," I reply, my chest tightening at the thought of the lives lost. "But we can't lose hope, Elena. Not now." Her eyes search mine, and for a moment, it feels as though we're the only two people left in the world. I reach out, brushing a finger along her arm, feeling the warmth of her skin beneath the rough fabric of her dress. "We have to find a way to fight back," I insist, my voice low and urgent. "Together." Elena's breath hitches, and I can see the conflict swirling within her. "What if we fail?" she whispers, her voice barely above a breath. "What if we lose everything?" "Then we lose everything together," I say, my heart pounding in my chest. "But I'd rather face that than live in a world without you."

Her eyes shimmer with unshed tears, and I can't help but reach for her, pulling her close. The warmth of her body against mine feels like a lifeline, grounding me in the chaos surrounding us. "You don't have to carry this alone," I murmur, my lips brushing against her forehead. "We can be each other's strength." For a heartbeat, the weight of the world slips away, and there's just Elena and me, two souls intertwining in the midst of a storm. But then reality crashes back in, the sounds of gunfire and the distant cries of the villagers reminding us of the danger lurking just beyond the walls of our sanctuary.

"I wish things were different," she breathes, pulling back to look into my eyes. "I wish we could just—" "Just what?" I ask, desperate for her to voice the thought hanging in the air. "Be free?" "Yes," she replies, her voice steadying. "To dream without fear. To love without boundaries." The intensity of her gaze ignites something deep within me. "Then let's make that our goal," I say, determination flooding my veins. "Let's dream together, even if it feels impossible right now. We'll find a way to fight for that freedom, for our love."

Elena nods slowly, a flicker of hope igniting in her eyes. "Together," she whispers, and in that moment, I feel the fragile threads of our connection weave tighter. I lean in, capturing her lips in a kiss that speaks of promises and dreams yet to be fulfilled. It's a kiss filled with the taste of desperation and longing, but also the sweet promise of hope. Beneath the weight of war, we find solace in each other, an anchor in the storm. And as we pull away, I know that no matter what the future holds, we have each other—and in this dark time, that is enough. The air crackles with tension, thick with the scent of smoke and the distant rumble of artillery.

I stand at the edge of the cave, peering out into the dimming light of dusk. The sun hangs low on the horizon, casting a bloody hue over the hills of Sicily. It's beautiful and horrific all at once. I can hear Elena's soft voice from behind me, soothing the frightened children huddled together, their wide eyes reflecting the fear that has become a near-constant companion in these dark times.

13

A Dangerous Mission

The sun hangs low in the sky, casting a golden hue over the rugged Sicilian landscape, but the serenity is a stark contrast to the turmoil brewing in my heart. I stand at the edge of the makeshift camp, the hum of distant planes echoing in my ears. Each drone of their engines feels like a call, a reminder of the duty I must fulfil even as I long to remain here, hidden away from the chaos, nestled within the embrace of this village and the woman who has come to mean everything to me. Elena is not far away, her figure framed against the backdrop of the hills, a silhouette of strength and resilience. She moves with purpose, gathering supplies from the villagers who look to her for guidance and comfort. I watch her, captivated by the way she interacts with them, her hands deftly weaving through the fabric of their fears, stitching hope into their hearts. But I know the danger looming over us is growing, and with it, the weight of my responsibilities.

The call to arms is not merely a summons to battle; it's an urgent plea that echoes in my soul, reminding me of my duty as a soldier. The Allied forces need every able man to push back against the German advance, and while I am grateful for the sanctuary this village has provided, I am painfully aware that I cannot hide forever. The military's need for reconnaissance has become critical, and I am one of the few left who can fulfil that role. The thought of leaving Elena behind, even for a short time, gnaws at me, twisting my stomach into knots.

I approach her, my footsteps silent on the jagged rocks as I try to mask my internal struggle. She senses my presence before I speak, turning to face me, her dark eyes searching mine for answers. "What is it, Jack?" she asks, her voice steady despite the uncertainty that looms between us. "There's a mission," I begin, the words feeling heavy on my tongue. "They need me to scout ahead, gather intel on the German positions. It could turn the tide for the Allied forces."

Her expression shifts, the flicker of fear crossing her features like a shadow passing over the sun. "But you could be captured, or worse." The tremble in her voice betrays her bravery, and I take a step closer, wanting to bridge the distance between us. "I know the risks, Elena. But if I don't go, how many more will suffer? This village… you… you could be in even greater danger if I don't do my part." I reach for her hand, intertwining my fingers with hers, feeling the warmth of her skin against mine. "I can't let that happen."

The silence stretches between us, thick and charged. She studies me, weighing my words, and I can see the battle waging within her, a desire to protect me clashing with her understanding of the greater good. "Jack," she finally whispers, her voice barely audible above the rustling leaves, "you are more than a soldier to me. You are… you are my heart." Her confession washes over me, a balm to my soul even in the face of impending danger. I squeeze her hand tighter, my resolve hardening. "And you are mine. But I have to do this. I can't stay here while others fight and die. I have to fight for you, for this village, for a future where we can be free of this nightmare." Tears shimmer in her eyes, and I can feel my own heart breaking at the sight. I want to promise her that I'll return, that I'll be back before she can even miss me, but the truth is, I can't make that promise. War is unpredictable, and fate is a fickle mistress.

All I can offer her is the truth of my feelings, my unwavering determination to protect her and the life we have begun to carve out together.

"Promise me you'll be careful," she implores, her voice trembling with emotion. "Promise me you'll come back." "I promise," I say, though the weight of that promise hangs heavy in the air. I lean in, brushing my lips against hers, a kiss that carries the weight of everything unspoken between us. It's a kiss filled with desperation and hope, the kind that lingers long after our lips part, igniting a fire within me that pushes back the fear. As I pull away, I can see the strength in her eyes, tempered by love but also by the harsh reality we face. "You're not just a soldier, Jack. You're a man I care deeply for. Don't forget that, even in the chaos." "I could never forget," I reply, my voice firm. "You are my anchor. I'll keep you in my heart, no matter where I go." With one last lingering glance, I turn away, my heart heavy yet resolute. I gather my gear, checking the revolver strapped to my thigh, feeling the comforting weight of it. Each step toward the makeshift command centre is both exhilarating and terrifying, the call to arms ringing in my ears like a drumbeat urging me forward.

The air is thick with tension as I approach my fellow pilots, their faces etched with determination. They are brothers in arms, each carrying their own burdens, yet united by a common purpose. We gather around a map spread out on a crude wooden table, the details of our mission laid bare. "Jack, you're leading the recon flight," the squadron leader says, his voice steady. "We need eyes on the ground, and you're the best man for the job. I trust you'll get us the intel we need." I nod, feeling the weight of responsibility settle on my shoulders. "I won't let you down," I assure him, though I can't shake the image of Elena's worried face from my mind.

We eventually finalize our plans, the reality of the mission sinks in. This isn't just about gathering information; it's about life and death, about the freedom of the people I've come to care for. I glance back toward the village, knowing that beneath the oppressive weight of war, a flicker of hope still burns brightly, sustained by the love I share with Elena. The call to arms has been made, and I am ready to answer it, if only to protect what I hold most dear. With one last deep breath, I steal myself for the flight ahead, prepared to face whatever challenges await me, driven by the love that fuels my spirit beneath the Sicilian sky. The sun hangs low in the sky, casting long shadows over the rugged terrain of Sicily. I stand at the edge of the village, the air thick with tension and the faint echoes of distant artillery. My heart pounds in my chest, a relentless reminder of the task ahead. I can't shake the feeling that time is slipping through my fingers like the grains of sand on the beach. The thought of leaving Elena behind gnaws at me, but duty calls, and I must answer. Elena's voice echoes in my mind, a soothing balm against the chaos surrounding us. She's been my anchor, my unwavering support amidst the uncertainty of war. I remember her laughter, bright and hopeful, a stark contrast to the dark clouds of despair that loom over our heads. I can't let her down; I can't let the people of this village down. They've sheltered me, offered me kindness in a time wrought with danger. I owe them everything.

As I gather my thoughts, the weight of my decisions presses heavily on my shoulders. The mission is dangerous, fraught with risks that could cost lives, including my own. But I can't ignore the intelligence we've gathered—the German forces are regrouping, and if we don't strike now, we might lose our chance to disrupt their operations. I glance back at the cave where Elena and the other villagers are huddled, their faces etched with worry, their eyes filled with fear. I need to protect them, to ensure their safety, and the only way to do that now is to take a stand. With a deep breath, I steal myself, drawing on the courage that has carried me through countless battles. I remember the look in Elena's eyes when I told her about the mission, the mix of fear and pride that danced across her features. She understands the stakes, the need for action. Yet, I can't help but wonder if she truly grasps how deeply I care for her, how my heart aches at the thought of leaving her behind again.

My determination solidifies as I prepare for the mission. I gather my gear, checking and double-checking my supplies. Each piece of equipment feels like a lifeline, a tangible reminder of the fight I'm about to undertake. I can't afford to falter; the lives of innocent people depend on my success. As I make my way to the designated meeting point, I feel the weight of the villagers' hope resting on my shoulders. They've placed their trust in me, a stranger from a distant land, and that trust fuels my resolve. I can't let them down. I can't let Elena down.

When I arrive at the meeting point, a small clearing surrounded by thick brush, I find my fellow squadron waiting. Their faces are grim, but there's a shared understanding that binds us together, our purpose unites us in this fight against tyranny. We exchange brief nods, our unspoken camaraderie a flicker of light in this dark time. "Jack," one of the sergeants calls out, his voice steady despite the tension in the air. "You ready for this? I nod, feeling the adrenaline coursing through my veins. "As ready as I'll ever be. We stick to the plan. No mistakes." The team gathers around, each airmen offering their own silent affirmation of the mission ahead. We go over the details again, timing, routes, potential enemy positions. I can feel the weight of their expectations, the responsibility of leadership pressing down on me.

"We'll move at dusk," I say, my voice firm. "We'll use the cover of darkness to get as close to their camp as possible. Once we're in position, we strike hard and fast. No hesitation." "Understood," one of the airmen replies, determination etched on his face. As we finalize our plans, I can't shake the image of Elena from my mind. I picture her standing in the village, her strong yet gentle spirit shining through even in the face of adversity. I want to tell her that I'll be back, that this isn't goodbye. But I can't afford to make promises I might not be able to keep. The thought of leaving her again, uncertain of what the dawn might bring, sends a shiver down my spine. Night falls, cloaking the landscape in shadows. I take a moment to breathe in the cool air, trying to calm the storm inside me. The stars begin to twinkle above, a beautiful reminder of the life that continues despite the war. I whisper a silent prayer for the villagers, for Elena, and for the strength to see this mission through. As I prepare to move into the cockpit of the aircraft, I catch one last glimpse of the cave in the distance.

The flicker of a candle illuminates the entrance, a beacon of hope in the darkness. I remind myself why I'm doing this—to protect those who cannot fight for themselves, to give them a chance at a future free from fear. The time has come. I set out, I am now silent against the earth, I am focused on the mission ahead. The weight of my determination pushes me forward, a fire igniting within me that I know will not be extinguished. I will fight for them, for Elena, and for the love that has blossomed amidst the chaos. As we fly and navigate the terrain, I feel a sense of purpose enveloping me. I am not just a pilot. I am a protector, a soldier, and a man driven by something greater than myself. I will do whatever it takes to ensure that the sun rises over Sicily once more, and that love—our love—can flourish beneath the Sicilian sky. The sun is low in the sky, casting a golden hue over the rugged Sicilian horizon. The air is thick with tension, a palpable silence settling over the village as I remember the villagers in the hidden cave we've called home for the past weeks. In my thoughts I can picture Elena standing beside me, her expression is a mix of determination and worry. I can't help but admire her strength, the way her eyes burn with resolve even in the face of danger.

Tonight, I must continue with my mission—one that feels both necessary and reckless. The German patrols have been growing bolder, moving closer to our refuge. If I don't act now, we risk losing everything. The villagers have become like family to me, and I won't let them fall into enemy hands. As I radio my other squadron leader I remind him of the importance of our mission., "Listen closely," I say, my voice steady despite the flutter of anxiety in my gut. "We need to help our friends on the ground gather supplies for our Allied forces. It's our best chance of getting help." An eerie sound ripples on the radio. I scan the squadron, remembering the laughter of the airmen and the warmth of shared meals. I can't let fear dictate our fate. My crew is already waiting for my further orders, Michael, Tom and Spencer. Hardened, weary, but ready. "They're advancing on the cave," I shout as I fly and climb nearby. "We've got to hit the Germans on the ground fast, and hard." Tom is flying beside me. "Been waiting for this."

The engines roar with us as we continue just as the first crackle of gunfire erupts from below. Our wings slice through the early morning sky, the rising sun gleaming off the metal hull. In the distance, smoke spirals into the air—Elena's signal. She made it. "All squadrons, form up!" I call over the radio, adjusting our heading. "Coordinates marked. We intercept now." A chorus of affirmatives replies. Seven bombers are strong. The full unit all airborne.

Then we see them, convoys of German trucks and infantry pushing toward the valley, their black cross insignia stark against the golden terrain. Tanks roll behind them, grinding over ancient stone paths like monsters in a dream. "Coming in hot," Martin calls from the nav station. "Target in range in ten seconds." "Bombs armed," Spencer says. "Fire on my mark… three, two, one—drop!" Payloads release. The first line of trucks explodes in a deafening roar. Flames spiral into the air. Enemy soldiers scatter, some firing upward blindly, others diving for cover. We bank hard to avoid the flak erupting from below. Tracer rounds zip past the fuselage. One nicks the wing—nothing critical. Not yet. The radio crackles. "They're pushing back—enemy fighters incoming, three o'clock!"

I twist in my seat to see them: Messerschmitt's diving in like hawks. Fast. Brutal.

"We're not letting them through," I growl. "Squadron,

engage." The sky becomes a war zone. Planes twist and roll in tight combat spirals. Explosions ripple across the valley. Our gunners return fire, tearing through enemy wings with merciless precision. A Messerschmitt spins out, smoke trailing behind it like a black comet before it slams into the hillside. But we take damage too. One of our bombers peels off, trailing flame. No chute. No time. My throat clenches. "We've got to hold them!" I shout. "Elena needs time!" I bank the plane low, heart pounding, engines screaming.

Below, I catch a flash of red, Elena, crossing open ground, shielded by villagers as they unload the supplies onto a flat clearing. They've built the signal. Bright. Visible from miles. "Elena's done her part," I breathe. "Now it's up to us." We go in for another pass. This time I aim to scatter the second German wave. Bomb doors open. More payloads drop. Boom. Boom. Smoke and dust churn up like thunderclouds. The Germans scatter. The valley holds. "Allied ground troops are inbound!" crackles the radio. "We've got friendlies pushing in from the south!" Relief crashes through me, almost knocking the air from my lungs. "Copy that," I say, eyes still locked on the burning horizon. "We'll cover until they arrive." We make one final sweep, strafing the last of the retreating enemy vehicles.

And then, slowly, the sky clears. The radio falls silent. Just the wind now. And the sky. We've done it. I bring the bomber around and circle the clearing one last time. Below, Elena stands with her hand raised, red cloth waving gently in the breeze. I tilt the wings side to side—our signal, just for her. I land just before noon. Dust kicks up around the tires as I climb out, legs shaking with exhaustion. She's already running toward me. I meet her halfway, and without a word, she throws her arms around me. "You came back," she says, voice muffled against my jacket. "I always will," I whisper, holding her tight. "You're my home now."

Around us, the villagers cheer. Allied jeeps roll in. For now, the valley is safe. And as I look into Elena's eyes—dusty, tear-filled, and radiant—I know we've done more than survive. We've carved a future out of fear. Together. The ground is warm beneath my knees, but I can't stop shaking. My arms are still wrapped around Elena's waist, holding her like she might vanish into the dust if I let her go. My heart beats steadily against hers. Alive. Still here. I made it back. "I told you I would," I say softly, while brushing my hair back. But we both know there was no guarantee. War doesn't make promises. I pull away enough to look at her. There's a smear of soot across my temple, a tear in the sleeve of my flight suit, blood drying on the edge of my collar. My eyes are bloodshot and tired, but alive—so very alive. "You held them back," she whispers. "And you delivered the signal," I reply. "We did it, Elena."

Around us, the villagers slowly begin to emerge from the cave. Some limp. Some weep. Children cling to mothers. One of the Allied soldiers hands a ration pack to a young girl, ruffling her hair. There's a strange hush in the air, like the world is exhaling all at once. For the first time in weeks, I can breathe.

But then my gaze falls to the hills. Smoke still curls into the sky. The price of what we've done is written in the scorched earth, the broken trees, and the still-burning remains of enemy trucks. "Come," Jack says gently. "Let's help with the wounded." We move from group to group—checking injuries, handing out water, giving comfort where we can. I tear strips of cloth from my undershirt to make bandages. I cradle a child with a twisted ankle. The villagers look to us now—not just as fighters, but as something more. Symbols, maybe. Or hope. Later, the commanding officer of the Allied detachment approaches us. His uniform is dust-covered, but he stands tall. He's seen what we've done. "We've set up a secure perimeter," he tells me. "This valley's under Allied control now. Supplies are inbound.

Medical aid too. I nod. "Thank you, sir." "We'll need to relocate the villagers. Safer inland. But what you did today…" He pauses, looking between us. "You bought them a future."

When the sun begins to set again, casting that familiar amber light across the Sicilian countryside, Jack and I walk out to the bluff above the village. The same place where he first told me about the mission. The same place I first began to understand just how much this war had taken from him—and how much he still had to give. "You still have your wings," I say, watching the sky. "But you're not just a pilot anymore." He's quiet for a long time, his hand brushing against mine. "You made me more than that." I turn to face him. "So… what happens now?"

I look out across the valley, where Allied jeeps roll like silent guardians beneath the clouds. Then I look at him. "We rebuild," I say. "We stay. Or go. Whatever you want. But I know one thing—I'm not flying away from this. Not from Elena and the children." Tears prick my eyes, but I smile. "Then stay. With us." Replies the Allied commander. I step closer. "Sure." I look for Elena in the crowd and kiss her; it's not rushed or desperate like those moments stolen between chaos and survival. It's slow. Real. Full of something deeper than I ever thought I'd feel in the middle of a war. Hope. Love. We stand there, arms wrapped around each other, as the stars begin to pierce through the dusk. For once, they shine not as reminders of what we've lost, but of what we've saved. And beneath this sky of hope, scarred and sacred, we begin again.

14

The Tides of Change

The planes are gone. The German bombs have stopped falling. But the silence they leave behind is just as heavy. The sky hangs grey above the valley, thick with ash and memory. The chapel still stands, though half its roof is missing. We've strung canvas across the beams to keep the sun off the children. It flaps gently in the wind, like a tired flag. For now, this is home. We were promised safety, and for a few days, it feels like we might have found it. The Allied trucks arrived at dawn—three of them, loaded with crates. Food, water, bandages. A field medic with soft eyes and a haunted look helped her carry the first wounded boy from the cave to the makeshift clinic inside what used to be the schoolhouse. There are seventeen children under her care now. Some lost their families in the last air raid. Some never had them to begin with. Lucia hasn't spoken in two days. Mateo clings to me like my shadow, flinching at every raised voice, every sudden sound.

We clean their wounds. We feed them. We sing to them at night. And still, it never feels like enough. She organizes the supplies with Maria's help. She moves like a ghost—quiet, efficient, always watching. She's not a child anymore. War aged her in ways I wish I could undo. We fill the old wine cellar with provisions: sacks of lentils and rice, cartons of dried milk, jugs of water. We stack tins and fold blankets, careful to ration fairly. The bandages go quickly. There are too many cuts, too many burns. The villagers trickle in slowly. Some of them haven't spoken since the bombing. Others talk too much—words tumbling out in fragments, stories with no beginning and no end. Elena listens to them all. They need to be heard. Even if I'm drowning inside. This afternoon, a baby was born. It should've been a moment of joy, but the mother cried through the whole thing—not from pain, but from fear.

She looked at me with glassy eyes and whispered, "Where will she grow up?" she didn't have an answer. But it's been weighing on her ever since. We're alive. Yes. We have food. Water. Medicine. A temporary peace. But peace is not the same as safety. The Germans haven't left Sicily. They've just repositioned. Regrouped. And if they return to the valley, and I know they willit will be worse than before. There will be no time to run. No caves left to hide in. We cannot stay. I stand in the chapel ruins that night, watching the flames of the cooking fire flicker across the stone walls. The children sleep in a tangled pile of limbs and blankets, their breathing shallow, their rest uneasy. She makes the decision as the wind carries the distant sound of thunder—not from a storm, but from artillery. We have to move. The next morning, she gathers the villagers in what's left of the square. A long scar of bomb damage cuts through the centre, like a warning.

"I know you're tired," she says. "And afraid. But we can't wait for the next attack to come. We need to go somewhere higher, somewhere out of reach." There's a low murmur of dissent. Some nod. Others frown. "Where would we even go?" asks Signora Mansi, cradling her toddler. "There's a ridge two days west," Elena replies. "Old shepherd trails. Forest cover. The Allies are setting up outposts there. They'll protect us." "And what if they don't?" someone calls out. she takes a breath. "Then we'll protect each other. Like we always have." It's not a rousing speech. But it's the truth. And slowly, they begin to agree. One by one, hands rise. One by one, we begin to hope again.

The children help us pack. Mateo tucks a tin soldier into his pocket. Lucia carries a folded drawing of her parents she's too scared to show anyone. Maria's inventories every item with careful precision. By nightfall, we're ready. We leave at first light, quietly, steadily, like shadows melting from the valley. I take one last look at the chapel, the bluff, the sky. He is out there somewhere. Fighting. Surviving. If she stays, she is risking everything we fought for. But if she leads them out… she gives them a chance.

She tucks the compass he gave her into her coat. And she begins to walk. Not away from him—but toward the life we both promised we'd fight to build. The trail winds upward through scorched olive groves and rocky brush, the dry wind brushing our faces like an old hand. We travel in silence at first. Not out of fear, though there is plenty of that—but because silence has become our language now. A shared breath. A steady footstep. The creak of a cartwheel. All speak louder than words. Elena walks at the front with Maria and two of the older men. Behind them, the villagers carry what little they can: food, blankets, and the hope that the next place won't fall to ash. The children stay close. She checks them constantly—Lucia with her drawing, Mateo clutching my coat, the three youngest walking hand-in-hand.

I try to smile at them when they look at me, but my mouth feels stiff. She hasn't slept in two days. The weight of leadership is heavier than fear. By midday, the heat is brutal. We stop under the shade of a crumbling stone wall—what's left of an abandoned farmhouse. The soldiers who promised to scout ahead haven't returned yet. She can feel the weight of every delay like a stone in her chest. The Germans are still out there. Maybe not today. Maybe not tomorrow. But we can't wait for another ambush to prove we were too slow. Elena shares the last of the figs she packed. Maria helps the younger one's drink from the water flask in turns. The villagers rest in the shade, murmuring softly. "I can carry more," Maria says loudly, Elena glances at her, face streaked with dust, her eyes wide open. Maria reminds her of herself when she first lost her home, my mother. She nods. "You already carry more than most." We move again before the sun begins to sink too low. The terrain grows harsher. Loose rocks. Steeper hills. Every few meters, someone stumbles.

Every few hours, someone weeps quietly, thinking no one hears. But we keep walking. Because there is no other choice. At dusk, we reach the ridge. The wind here is sharp and cold, and the view below reveals the full shape of what we left behind: smoke trails still rising from the valley, rooftops crushed like tin under the heel of war. Some fall to their knees, overwhelmed. She doesn't. She holds herself steady. Because they are watching her. Because Jack would want her to keep going. Because this is not where we stop. We make camp near a rocky outcrop, half-sheltered by trees. The Allies said there was a safe checkpoint here, and just before nightfall, she spots it, a flicker of movement in the woods, the flash of a signal mirror. British troops. We're guided to a secured clearing with canvas tents, crates of supplies, and a medical station.

She counts the children again as they pass through—every one of them accounted for. Every soul we carried from the valley made it through the journey. Relief hits her so hard she nearly drops to the ground. One of the medics takes her arm. "You led them here?" he asks, astonished. "I just walked," she says, dazed. "No. You carried them." That night, she sits by the campfire, bandaging a blister on Mateo's foot while Maria and the others help distribute food. The air is cooler up here, and the stars feel closer, brighter, sharper. She looks up, wondering if Jack can see them from wherever he is. Wondering if he's still alive. And somehow, she believes he is. He has to be. Because she didn't come all this way just to rebuild a village. She came here so he'd have something to return to.

Just before dawn, a jeep arrives at the edge of the checkpoint, dust trailing behind it like a promise. A dispatch officer jumps out, handing something to the lieutenant at the gate. He glances at it, then turns and scans the camp. "Elena Santoro?" she rises slowly. "Here." He hands her a slip of paper. It's damp with dew, but the ink is fresh. **Captain Jack Branner's aircraft has returned safely. Minor injuries. He requests confirmation of your arrival at the ridge. Response requested immediately.** The world tilts slightly. He's alive. He made it back. Her hands tremble, but she presses the reply into the officer's hand with a firm nod. "Tell him, "Her voice steady, "that I'm here." And I'll wait—for as long as it takes. The days blur. They have been at the ridge camp for a couple of days now. It's safer here higher, surrounded by Allied patrols, with thick trees that muffle sound and hide movement. Still, she does not let the children stray too far. Safety feels like a borrowed thing, something temporary, something fragile. Thay have built tents from tarpaulins and wood. The British engineers set up a small field kitchen and a rotating watchtower. At night, the soldiers take turns standing guard while the rest of us sleep, uneasy but undisturbed.

Each morning, she is woken to the sound of birds again. Real birds. Singing. The first time she heard them, she cried. The children are adjusting. Lucia smiles now when she draws. Mateo plays with a small carved plane a soldier whittled for him. Maria helps the medics daily, tending wounds with practiced care. She speaks less, but when she does, people listen. She is becoming what she once was— before the bombings, before she lost everything but her name and her will. A new identity is forming here, not just for Elena, but for all of them. They are no longer just survivors of a ruined village. They are a community. One evening, the lieutenant in charge approaches Elena. His hands are tucked behind his back, his uniform crisp despite the heat. "You've done more here in six days than we've seen in six weeks elsewhere," he says. "The children trust you. So do the civilians. If you'd be willing, I'd like to recommend you for liaison duty between our logistics team and the displaced refugees."

She blinks. "Me? I'm not a soldier." "No. You're better. You're a leader." The word hits me like a stone she didn't know she was carrying. Leader. Not by choice, but by necessity. She nods, slowly. "If it helps them... I'll do it." He smiles. "Then we'll start tomorrow." Still, every evening when my work is done, she climbs the narrow path above the camp. There's a boulder up there with a view west— toward the airstrip. Toward the skies, she sits on that stone and looks for him for Jack.

Each day, she receives another field update. "Captain Jack Branner assisting with aerial relief supply drops." "Branner assigned to recon patrol over coastal villages." "Branner last seen at forward base Delta, due back in 48 hours." He's close. So close. But not here. She tells herself to be patient. War doesn't bend to hearts. It bends to strategy. Orders. Fuel lines. Wind. Still... she keeps watching. Still... she waits. It's the ninth evening when it happens.

She is washing linen by the camp's spring when she hears the familiar growl of a plane overhead—not fast and screaming like the fighter craft, but slower… heavier. She freezes, hands dripping, heart stammering in my chest. The plane banks low once, just enough for her to catch it clearly through the treetops. A twin-engine bomber. Familiar silhouette. A flicker of silver on its underside, painted initials. **JB.** Jack Branner. Her legs move before she thinks. She runs. Through the camp, past stunned soldiers and calling voices. She takes the trail to the overlook at full speed, her lungs burning. And there, through the clouds breaking open into dusky orange light, she sees the plane begin its descent toward the airfield in the valley below.

I am back. This time, she doesn't just watch. By the time she reaches the edge of the clearing, dust is still settling around the aircraft's wheels. Mechanics are already running out with fuel carts. The crew is climbing down, stretching, joking. And then she sees me. Bruised. Dirty. Alive. My helmet is off, flight jacket half-open. There's a bandage on my left hand. But my eyes search the airstrip like I am looking for someone. Like I already know she is here. "Jack!" Elena shouts, unable to hold back. My head snaps toward the sound. And then I run. She meets me halfway across the field. She doesn't remember how long we hold onto each other. There's dust in my eyes, tears on my flight suit, my hand cupped behind my neck like he needs to be sure I'm real. "I found you," I whispers. "You always do." That night, we sit at the edge of the campfire, my arm wrapped tightly around her, her head resting on my shoulder. The stars above us are clear and steady. "I saw what you did," I murmur. "Bringing them here. Keeping them alive." "I only did what I could."

I turn to her, my voice fierce and soft all at once. "You did more than survive. You carried everyone else with you." she swallows the lump in her throat. "We still have so far to go," she whispers. "I know." I reach into my jacket and presses the compass I gave her back into her palm. "But now we go together." The stars don't look the same up here. They're clearer. Closer. Like I could pluck one out of the sky and hand it to her if she asked. Elena's head rests against my shoulder, her breath warm against my collarbone. She hasn't said much since we sat down. Neither have I. We don't need to. We're both too tired to waste words on things we already know. She's alive. I'm alive. And somehow, after everything, we found each other again. I let out a slow breath, the tension finally leaving my body in pieces. The mission's behind me. For now. No more gunfire. No smoke trails or evasive manoeuvres or maps marked with red ink. Just the sound of wind through pine trees and the crackle of a campfire.

Her fingers brush mine. I take her hand and don't let go. The next morning, I wake before sunrise. Old habit. Elena's still asleep beside me, curled beneath a canvas blanket. I watch her for a moment, the rise and fall of her chest, the strand of hair over her cheek, the faint crease between her brows like even in sleep, she's carrying too much. She led them here. I'd heard rumours, field notes, brief mentions from soldiers: "The civilians were guided out by a young woman—Elena something." I didn't believe it until I read the report myself. She saved them. All of them. Without weapons. Without orders. Just instinct, heart, and iron will. I've dropped bombs over cities. I've led missions through flak and fire. But what she did... what she endured... That's something else. That's real courage.

By midday, the camp is alive with movement. Children chasing each other between tents. Villagers stacking crates and drying clothes on lines strung between trees. A group of Allied engineers work on fortifying the trail. I walk through the camp with a tin mug of weak coffee and nod to familiar faces—some I've flown with; some I've only seen from the air. "Elena's up by the supply tents," Maria tells me, pointing with her chin. "Don't let her carry everything herself again." I smile. "No promises." When I find her, she's organizing bandages with one hand and comforting a crying child with the other. The moment she sees me, something in her posture softens. "You're walking like you didn't just fly two back-to-back missions," she says, arching an eyebrow. "You're talking like you didn't just lead a civilian convoy through a warzone." She hands me a crate of gauze. "Then I guess we're even."

We spend the day working side by side. We rebuild storage. Check injuries. Distribute soap and water rations. She's tireless, focused, calm in the chaos. At one point, I catch her watching a young mother rock her newborn under the shade of a canvas awning. Her expression twists—grief, wonder, something in between. "You, okay?" I ask quietly. She nods. "They deserve better than this." "We all do." Later, we sit on a fallen log near the edge of the ridge. Below us, the valley stretches wide and green again, its wounds slowly healing. "I used to think flying was everything," I admit. "The speed, the precision, the control. But now…" "But now?" she echoes. I look at her, really look at her. "Now I think all of that was just leading me to you." She doesn't answer right away. Then she leans in, forehead resting gently against mine. "Then don't fly away again." "I won't," I whisper. "Not unless you're flying with me."

Beneath a Sky of Hope

The Allied commander calls me in that evening. He says there's talk of a permanent relocation—moving the civilians north, away from the combat zones entirely. Safer, but colder. Farther from home. He wants my input. I say I'll speak to Elena. But I already know what she'll say. This camp isn't a place. It's a promise. A fragile beginning rooted in ash and stitched together by grit, care, and love.

And for the first time in a long time, I think I'm ready to stop running and help it grow.

Something is wrong. I can feel it in the way the air shifts, too still, too quiet. The kind of quiet that doesn't last. The kind that comes before a rifle shot. I'm at the edge of the camp, boots in the dirt, rifle slung low, watching the trees. The suns just dipped behind the ridge, casting long shadows across the hilltops. The children are in the shelter with Elena. The guards are posted. Supplies are stacked. We're as ready as we can be. But that doesn't mean we're safe. I step forward slowly, checking the line of trees again. Then I smell it—smoke. Cigarette. Not ours. And I hear it. The crack of a twig. Two voices, low, clipped German. They're closer than I thought. Scouts. I duck low, motioning to the nearest guard. He sees me and nods. One hand on his weapon. The other steadying his breath. I backtrack fast, my boots silent in the dirt, and head for command. We've got company.

The commander listens with a grim expression. "How many?" "Two, maybe three. Could be more behind them." "You think it's a probe?" I nod. "Small unit. Testing for weakness. They'll come back stronger." He rubs a hand over his face. "We're stretched thin." "I know. But we can't afford to wait for a full assault." "Agreed." "Let me get Elena and the children into the shelter. Deeper." "Do it. Quietly. We don't need panic." I'm already gone. By the time I reach the medical tent, Elena's already in motion. She knows. I don't even have to say it. Her eyes find mine, calm and steady, like always.

"How long do we have?" "An hour. Maybe less." "Then we move now." She doesn't flinch. Doesn't cry. Just grabs her bag, calls Ana, and starts directing people with that quiet voice that somehow cuts through fear like a knife. I help carry the smallest boy—Samuel, the one who hasn't spoken since his parents died. His arms go around my neck like he's always belonged there. One by one, we move them—into the old root cellar beneath the chapel ruin. Narrow. Musty. Cold. But safe.

We place the children in rows, tucked under blankets, pressed together like embers in a fire that refuses to go out.

Beneath a Sky of Hope

Elena kneels in the dark with them, whispering something I can't quite hear. They stop trembling. She has that effect on people. She's the strongest person I've ever known. We hold our breath as the sun disappears entirely. Then it starts. A single shot rings out—sharp and close. Then another. Soldiers scramble for cover. Shouts in German echo through the trees. Someone fires back. The camp erupts. I grab my rifle, sprint toward the south line, duck behind a stone wall. Flashes of muzzle fire light up the tree line. One of our men goes down. Another returns fire from a sandbag post. I fire twice—hit one silhouette. Then another. They're not expecting resistance. They thought we'd scatter. They were wrong.

The trees fall silent again. I wait. Breathing hard. Listening. Then... retreating footsteps. They're pulling back. This wasn't an ambush. This was a message. A warning. They'll be back—with more. After it's over, I walk through the camp. Four injured. One dead. A woman from the village, stray bullet through the chest. We bury her beside the others at dawn. I help dig the grave with numb hands. When I finish, I find Elena sitting against the chapel wall, head bowed, arms wrapped around Mateo. He's asleep. She isn't. I kneel beside her. She looks up at me—eyes red, face streaked with dust and tears that have dried where they fell.

She doesn't speak. Neither do I. I just wrap an arm around her and hold on. Because I know what she's thinking. They'll come again.

And this camp won't hold. By the time the sun breaks over the ridge, we've made our decision. Elena stands beside me, shoulders square, jaw set. "We move," she says. "Before they regroup. "There's a monastery," I tell her. "North. Built into the cliffs. Old, solid. Defensible." She nods once. "Then that's where we go." I look at the camp one last time. The makeshift tents. The field stove. The stone wall we fought from. Smoke still drifts from the edge of the trees. But there's nothing left here to protect. Only people. Only each other. And so, we leave. Not in defeat. But in defiance. The planes are gone. The German bombs have stopped falling. But the silence they leave behind is just as heavy. The sky hangs grey above the valley, thick with ash and memory. The chapel still stands, though half its roof is missing. We've strung canvas across the beams to keep the sun off the children. It flaps gently in the wind, like a tired flag. For now, this is home. We were promised safety, and for a few days, it feels like we might have found it.

The Allied trucks arrived at dawn—three of them, loaded with crates. Food, water, bandages. We leave just before sunset. Not because it's safer, but because daylight makes us a target. The trees will hide us. The hills will slow us, but they'll shield us too. I carry a rifle slung across my back and a map folded tight in my vest pocket, already soaked with sweat. Elena walks just behind me with the children. Maria comes close at the rear, quiet and alert.

The villagers move like they've been here before—which they have. Some are still limping. One carries an infant swaddled in bandages. But no one complains. There's no room left for that. We've burned through pain and fear and grief. All that's left is resolve. And survival. The terrain is worse than I remember. What used to be footpaths are now just scars in the hillside, mud, broken stone, undergrowth thick with briars. Every step cut into our progress. Every hour we fall further behind the clock I've built in my head—the one ticking down until the Germans find us again.

We take breaks when we can. Not long. Just enough for water, some rationed bread, and a whispered story from Elena to calm the children. They all gather around her like she's the sun, and maybe she is. The only steady warmth left in this fractured world. She catches my eye while she cradles Mateo, who's already half-asleep in her lap. She asks me. "You, okay?" I nod, even though I'm not. But I will be. Because she needs me to be. At the halfway mark, we reach the river crossing. Or what used to be a crossing. The bridge is gone. Washed out or blown up. I can't tell. All that's left is a broken plank angled over rushing water and a series of jagged stones jutting from the current like broken teeth.

Behind us, too far to see, but close enough to feel, I know they're moving. The Germans. Tracking us. Maybe not tonight. Maybe not even tomorrow. But soon. I can't afford to turn back. "Elena," I call, moving to her side, lowering my voice. "We're going to have to cross here." She glances at the water, then at the children. "All of them?" she asks. "All of us." Her face tightens, but she nods. "We go slow," she says. "You lead. I'll help them one by one." I test the stones first. My boots slip once, catch again. The water's cold and fast, but not deep enough to drag me.

I get across in thirty seconds, waving to the others once I'm stable on the far side. Then I go back. Again. And again. Child by child. Lucia's handshakes so badly I have to carry her halfway. Mateo clings to me, refusing to look down. Maria crosses last, soaking wet but grinning. "I hate rivers," she mutters. "We're clear," I call. Then I look at Elena. She's still on the other side. She's waiting for everyone else to go first. I motion for her. She doesn't move. "Elena," I say, firmer. "Come on." She steps onto the plank, arms out for balance. She's done this kind of thing before—I can tell. Every step calculated. But when she reaches the last stone, it shifts under her. "Jack," she gasps. I'm already moving.

I grab her arm just as the stone tips, and we fall together, landing in the icy shallows on our knees. Water surges over our legs. She coughs once, then laughs breathlessly, her arms around my neck. "You always catch me," she whispers. I pull her up and wrap her in my coat. "Always." We walk the last five miles in silence. The moon breaks through the clouds just as the monastery appears through the trees. Stone towers. Worn paths. Ancient, weather-beaten walls. But it's there. Still standing. I feel something ease in my chest. We made it. We get everyone inside—slowly, carefully. The children fall asleep in empty cloisters, curled into one another like leaves. The villagers set up what they can: blankets, lanterns, food crates. I scout the upper levels. The walls are solid. High. There's even an old well in the rear courtyard. Enough to keep us going.

When I return to the main hall, Elena's lighting candles in a stone alcove. Her hands are shaking. I move to her and place mine over hers. "We're here," I say. She nods, but her voice is barely a whisper. "I'm so tired, Jack." "I know." I wrap her in my arms and hold her there. She leans into me and closes her eyes. And we stand like that in the quiet dark—two people who've outrun death again, who've carried others on their backs, who've burned and bled and broken just to reach this place. A sanctuary. For now.

And maybe, if we're lucky, a new beginning. The monastery holds the cold like a memory. Thick stone walls. Arched ceilings. Empty halls that echo with every step. It smells like damp stone, old incense, and forgotten prayers. The wind cuts through broken windows, brushing through the ruins like it remembers the monks who once whispered here. But it's dry. Defensible. Hidden. It's hope, built out of rock. The villagers settle quickly, too quickly. That's what fear does. It teaches people how to adapt fast or die faster. Within the hour, someone has a fire going in the main chamber. Blankets are laid. A watch is assigned.

Elena moves through the space like she's lived here for years. She doesn't bark orders; she just makes things happen. I watch her wrap Lucia in a coat and tuck her close to Ana. She checks an old corridor for leaks. She ties Mateo's shoe. She hasn't eaten since we arrived. Neither have I. I spend the morning checking the perimeter. There's an old bell tower still standing, barely, but it gives a view of the entire ridge. From here I can see the trail we took, the forest behind it, and the snaking shadow of the river that almost took Elena from me two nights ago. I press the scope of my rifle to my eye. Clear. But I don't trust it. Not yet. Not ever, really. By midday, I've located a working well behind the north wing. I draw the first bucket myself, cold and clean. Elena meets me there, sleeves rolled up, dirt on her face. Her eyes are darker than usual. Not with fear. With fatigue.

I hand her the tin cup. She drinks like she hasn't in days. "How bad is it?" she asks between sips. "The walls are solid. No real cover in the back, but if we seal the chapel door and keep scouts posted, we can hold it." "For how long?" I shrug. "Long enough." She nods. "That'll have to do." I watch her a moment longer. She's fraying at the edges. I can see it, barely held together with grit and willpower. But she won't break. She'll bend, and she'll carry the weight again. For them. For us. "Elena," I say softly. She turns to me. "You don't have to do it alone." Something in her shoulder's eases. Just a little. She nods once. "I know. But it still feels like I do." That night, I sit on the edge of the courtyard, polishing the rifle I haven't fired since the river.

The wind howls through the cloisters. Somewhere above, the stars burn steady through the cracks in the stone ceiling. Elena joins me, wrapping a wool blanket around her shoulders. She doesn't say anything at first. Just leans into my side, rests her head against my shoulder. We sit like that for a long time. Then she whispers, "What if this is all we get? Just one quiet place between storms?" I look at her. The firelight dances in her eyes. "Then I'll take it," I say. "I'll take it, and I'll defend it with everything I have." She closes her eyes. "Me too." Later, when the children are asleep and the fire has burned down low, she reaches for my hand. And just like that, we become part of the stone. Part of this place. Not running. Not hiding. Just here. Building something worth staying for. Something we can fight for, if it comes to that. And we both know it will. But not tonight. Tonight, we rest.

15

Shadows at the Edge

Something is wrong. I can feel it in the way the air shifts, too still, too quiet. The kind of quiet that doesn't last. The kind that comes before a rifle shot. I'm at the edge of the camp, boots in the dirt, rifle slung low, watching the trees. The suns just dipped behind the ridge, casting long shadows across the hilltops. The children are in the shelter with Elena. The guards are posted. Supplies are stacked. We're as ready as we can be. But that doesn't mean we're safe. I step forward slowly, checking the line of trees again. Then I smell it—smoke. Cigarette. Not ours. And I hear it. The crack of a twig. Two voices, low, clipped German. They're closer than I thought. Scouts. I duck low, motioning to the nearest guard. He sees me and nods. One hand on his weapon. The other steadying his breath. I backtrack fast, my boots silent in the dirt, and head for command. We've got company.

The commander listens with a grim expression. "How many?" "Two, maybe three. Could be more behind them." "You think it's a probe?" I nod. "Small unit. Testing for weakness. They'll come back stronger." He rubs a hand over his face. "We're stretched thin." "I know. But we can't afford to wait for a full assault." "Agreed." "Let me get Elena and the children into the shelter. Deeper." "Do it. Quietly. We don't need panic." I'm already gone. By the time I reach the medical tent, Elena's already in motion. She knows. I don't even have to say it. Her eyes find mine, calm and steady, like always.

"How long do we have?" "An hour. Maybe less." "Then we move now." She doesn't flinch. Doesn't cry. Just grabs her bag, calls Ana, and starts directing people with that quiet voice that somehow cuts through fear like a knife. I help carry the smallest boy—Samuel, the one who hasn't spoken since his parents died. His arms go around my neck like he's always belonged there. One by one, we move them—into the old root cellar beneath the chapel ruin. Narrow. Musty. Cold. But safe.

We place the children in rows, tucked under blankets, pressed together like embers in a fire that refuses to go out. Elena kneels in the dark with them, whispering something I can't quite hear. They stop trembling. She has that effect on people. She's the strongest person I've ever known. We hold our breath as the sun disappears entirely. Then it starts. A single shot rings out—sharp and close. Then another. Soldiers scramble for cover. Shouts in German echo through the trees. Someone fires back. The camp erupts. I grab my rifle, sprint toward the south line, duck behind a stone wall. Flashes of muzzle fire light up the tree line. One of our men goes down. Another returns fire from a sandbag post. I fire twice—hit one silhouette. Then another. They're not expecting resistance. They thought we'd scatter. They were wrong.

The trees fall silent again. I wait. Breathing hard. Listening. Then... retreating footsteps. They're pulling back. This wasn't an ambush. This was a message. A warning. They'll be back—with more. After it's over, I walk through the camp. Four injured. One dead. A woman from the village, stray bullet through the chest. We bury her beside the others at dawn. I help dig the grave with numb hands. When I finish, I find Elena sitting against the chapel wall, head bowed, arms wrapped around Mateo. He's asleep. She isn't. I kneel beside her. She looks up at me—eyes red, face streaked with dust and tears that have dried where they fell. She doesn't speak. Neither do I. I just wrap an arm around her and hold on. Because I know what she's thinking. They'll come again.

And this camp won't hold. By the time the sun breaks over the ridge, we've made our decision. Elena stands beside me, shoulders square, jaw set. "We move," she says. "Before they regroup. "There's a monastery," I tell her. "North. Built into the cliffs. Old, solid. Defensible." She nods once. "Then that's where we go." I look at the camp one last time. The makeshift tents. The field stove. The stone wall we fought from. Smoke still drifts from the edge of the trees. But there's nothing left here to protect. Only people. Only each other. And so, we leave. Not in defeat. But in defiance. The planes are gone. The German bombs have stopped falling. But the silence they leave behind is just as heavy. The sky hangs grey above the valley, thick with ash and memory. The chapel still stands, though half its roof is missing. We've strung canvas across the beams to keep the sun off the children. It flaps gently in the wind, like a tired flag. For now, this is home. We were promised safety, and for a few days, it feels like we might have found it.

The Allied trucks arrived at dawn—three of them, loaded with crates. Food, water, bandages. We leave just before sunset. Not because it's safer, but because daylight makes us a target. The trees will hide us. The hills will slow us, but they'll shield us too. I carry a rifle slung across my back and a map folded tight in my vest pocket, already soaked with sweat. Elena walks just behind me with the children. Maria comes close at the rear, quiet and alert.

The villagers move like they've been here before—which they have. Some are still limping. One carries an infant swaddled in bandages. But no one complains. There's no room left for that. We've burned through pain and fear and grief. All that's left is resolve. And survival. The terrain is worse than I remember. What used to be footpaths are now just scars in the hillside, mud, broken stone, undergrowth thick with briars. Every step cut into our progress. Every hour we fall further behind the clock I've built in my head—the one ticking down until the Germans find us again.

We take breaks when we can. Not long. Just enough for water, some rationed bread, and a whispered story from

Elena to calm the children. They all gather around her like she's the sun, and maybe she is. The only steady warmth left in this fractured world. She catches my eye while she cradles Mateo, who's already half-asleep in her lap. She asks me. "You, okay?" I nod, even though I'm not. But I will be. Because she needs me to be. At the halfway mark, we reach the river crossing. Or what used to be a crossing. The bridge is gone. Washed out or blown up. I can't tell. All that's left is a broken plank angled over rushing water and a series of jagged stones jutting from the current like broken teeth.

Behind us, too far to see, but close enough to feel, I know they're moving. The Germans. Tracking us. Maybe not tonight. Maybe not even tomorrow. But soon. I can't afford to turn back. "Elena," I call, moving to her side, lowering my voice. "We're going to have to cross here." She glances at the water, then at the children. "All of them?" she asks. "All of us." Her face tightens, but she nods. "We go slow," she says. "You lead. I'll help them one by one." I test the stones first. My boots slip once, catch again. The water's cold and fast, but not deep enough to drag me.

I get across in thirty seconds, waving to the others once I'm stable on the far side. Then I go back. Again. And again. Child by child. Lucia's handshakes so badly I have to carry her halfway. Mateo clings to me, refusing to look down. Maria crosses last, soaking wet but grinning. "I hate rivers," she mutters. "We're clear," I call. Then I look at Elena. She's still on the other side. She's waiting for everyone else to go first. I motion for her. She doesn't move. "Elena," I say, firmer. "Come on." She steps onto the plank, arms out for balance. She's done this kind of thing before—I can tell. Every step calculated. But when she reaches the last stone, it shifts under her. "Jack," she gasps. I'm already moving.

I grab her arm just as the stone tips, and we fall together, landing in the icy shallows on our knees. Water surges over our legs. She coughs once, then laughs breathlessly, her arms around my neck. "You always catch me," she whispers. I pull her up and wrap her in my coat. "Always." We walk the last five miles in silence. The moon breaks through the clouds just as the monastery appears through the trees. Stone towers. Worn paths. Ancient, weather-beaten walls. But it's there. Still standing. I feel something ease in my chest. We made it. We get everyone inside—slowly, carefully. The children fall asleep in empty cloisters, curled into one another like leaves. The villagers set up what they can: blankets, lanterns, food crates. I scout the upper levels. The walls are solid. High. There's even an old well in the rear courtyard. Enough to keep us going.

When I return to the main hall, Elena's lighting candles in a stone alcove. Her hands are shaking. I move to her and place mine over hers. "We're here," I say. She nods, but her voice is barely a whisper. "I'm so tired, Jack." "I know." I wrap her in my arms and hold her there. She leans into me and closes her eyes. And we stand like that in the quiet dark—two people who've outrun death again, who've carried others on their backs, who've burned and bled and broken just to reach this place. A sanctuary. For now.

And maybe, if we're lucky, a new beginning. The monastery holds the cold like a memory. Thick stone walls. Arched ceilings. Empty halls that echo with every step. It smells like damp stone, old incense, and forgotten prayers. The wind cuts through broken windows, brushing through the ruins like it remembers the monks who once whispered here. But it's dry. Defensible. Hidden. It's hope, built out of rock. The villagers settle quickly, too quickly. That's what fear does. It teaches people how to adapt fast or die faster. Within the hour, someone has a fire going in the main chamber. Blankets are laid. A watch is assigned.

Elena moves through the space like she's lived here for years. She doesn't bark orders; she just makes things happen. I watch her wrap Lucia in a coat and tuck her close to Ana. She checks an old corridor for leaks. She ties Mateo's shoe. She hasn't eaten since we arrived. Neither have I. I spend the morning checking the perimeter. There's an old bell tower still standing, barely, but it gives a view of the entire ridge. From here I can see the trail we took, the forest behind it, and the snaking shadow of the river that almost took Elena from me two nights ago. I press the scope of my rifle to my eye. Clear. But I don't trust it. Not yet. Not ever, really. By midday, I've located a working well behind the north wing. I draw the first bucket myself, cold and clean. Elena meets me there, sleeves rolled up, dirt on her face. Her eyes are darker than usual. Not with fear. With fatigue.

I hand her the tin cup. She drinks like she hasn't in days. "How bad is it?" she asks between sips. "The walls are solid. No real cover in the back, but if we seal the chapel door and keep scouts posted, we can hold it." "For how long?" I shrug. "Long enough." She nods. "That'll have to do." I watch her a moment longer. She's fraying at the edges. I can see it, barely held together with grit and willpower. But she won't break. She'll bend, and she'll carry the weight again. For them. For us. "Elena," I say softly. She turns to me. "You don't have to do it alone." Something in her shoulder's eases. Just a little. She nods once. "I know. But it still feels like I do." That night, I sit on the edge of the courtyard, polishing the rifle I haven't fired since the river.

The wind howls through the cloisters. Somewhere above, the stars burn steady through the cracks in the stone ceiling. Elena joins me, wrapping a wool blanket around her shoulders. She doesn't say anything at first. Just leans into my side, rests her head against my shoulder. We sit like that for a long time. Then she whispers, "What if this is all we get? Just one quiet place between storms?" I look at her. The firelight dances in her eyes. "Then I'll take it," I say. "I'll take it, and I'll defend it with everything I have." She closes her eyes. "Me too." Later, when the children are asleep and the fire has burned down low, she reaches for my hand. And just like that, we become part of the stone. Part of this place. Not running. Not hiding. Just here. Building something worth staying for. Something we can fight for, if it comes to that. And we both know it will. But not tonight. Tonight, we rest.

16

The Sound of Something New

The messages plays again. And again. And again. Each time, Elena stays beside me, standing, her eyes locked on the radio like she's afraid it'll disappear. "Repeat: Axis withdrawal confirmed. Allied forces crossing inland corridors with minimal resistance. Civilian zones secured. Reinforcements arriving from Malta and North Africa. Sicily is being liberated." The words crackle over old static, but they land clear. This isn't a rumour. This isn't a maybe. It's real. Elena exhales slowly, like she's been holding her breath for months. Maybe she has. "I never thought I'd hear something like this again," she whispers. I look at her, really look at her, and for the first time in too long I don't just see the fight in her. I see the girl beneath it. The one who once believed in spring and music and fresh bread and stories at dusk. And I swear—just for a moment—she looks lighter. Not happy. Not yet. But no longer hunted.

Later that night, we sit in the bell tower with the radio between us and a blanket wrapped over our shoulders. Below us, the monastery glows warm with firelight. Children laugh. Someone's cooking lentils. A soldier hums an old Italian folk tune. And above us, the stars. Elena's fingers trace a crack in the stone floor, absently, like she's learning it by touch. "They're going to come back," she says after a long silence. "The Germans?" "No. The others. People. Survivors. Families who hid in the woods. Refugees from the coasts. We'll see them soon. You'll see." She says it like a promise. And I believe her. "We'll be ready," I tell her. She nods, then turns to me. Her eyes are glassy in the moonlight. "Do you think we'll get to live a normal life after this?" I smile. "I think whatever life we live will be better if you're in it." Her brow furrows. "You always answer like a storybook." "That's because you're the only real ending I want." She lets out a soft laugh and leans into my side.

I wrap my arm around her, and we sit like that as the radio plays on. "...Enemy surrender expected soon. Allied posts reaching the western hills. Sicily's skies are clear..." She tilts her head up to look at me. "We survived," she whispers. "More than that," I say. "We found something worth surviving for." Then I kiss her. It's not rushed or desperate like it was in the caves. It's slow. Still. Honest. Her hand finds the back of my neck. My fingers settle over her heart. It's beating fast, and mine matches it, like two old clocks trying to find the same rhythm again. When we break apart, she's smiling for the first time in what feels like years. "You'll stay?" she asks. "There's nowhere else I'd rather be." We sit there until the radio goes quiet, the batteries draining to nothing. But the silence it leaves behind isn't empty. It's peace. The beginning of it, anyway. And if the world ever dares to rebuild, I want to start here—with her. Something is wrong. I can feel it in the way the air shifts— too still, too quiet. The kind of quiet that doesn't last. The kind that comes before a rifle shot. I'm at the edge of the camp, boots in the dirt, rifle slung low, watching the trees.

The sun just dipped behind the ridge, casting long shadows across the hilltops. The children are in the shelter with Elena. The guards are posted. Supplies are stacked. We're as ready as we can be. But that doesn't mean we're safe. The radio dies a few hours later. Batteries drained. No replacement in sight. We keep the set anyway. I set it on a table in the chapel beneath a cracked window where the sun pours in each morning. No one speaks about it, but we all glance at it now and then—like it might come back to life. Like it might say something new. But it's already done its job. We heard the news. And now they're coming. The first to arrive is a family of four—dusty, gaunt, cautious. The father limps, the mother holds a baby, the two children follow behind like shadows. Elena meets them outside the gate. She doesn't ask questions. She just says, "You're safe now," and leads them inside. I watch from the tower as they sit near the fire. Mateo gives one of the new boys a toy plane without saying a word. An hour later, more arrive. By nightfall, there are seventeen new faces inside the monastery. At the end of a couple of days—forty-six.

We open the western courtyard and clear the old cloisters. Elena draws maps on the stone with charcoal, marking spaces for sleeping quarters, a schoolroom, even a garden once the frost lifts. She's building something here, brick by invisible brick. People call her by name now. Not just Elena. "Signorina Elena." "Elena, what do you need?" "Elena said we'll be safe." I step back sometimes just to watch her move through the space, quiet, clear, kind. The war took everything from her, and still, she offers what she has left. She never demands. Never falters. Never turns anyone away. This isn't just a sanctuary. It's becoming a village again. And she's the reason.

We sit together one evening, legs dangling from the monastery wall. Below us, children run through the tall grass, their laughter filling the air like music. Someone's cooking with garlic again. The whole place smells like bread and second chances. Elena leans into me, her shoulder warm against mine. "They're saying the Germans won't come back," she says softly. "Not here. Not to Sicily." I nod.

"They won't." "But we still have to rebuild everything. Roads. Homes. A future." "We will," I say. She looks at me, brow raised. "You really believe that?" I smile. "I believe in you. That's more than enough." She laughs, just a little, and rests her head on my shoulder. I think about the girl I first saw handing out water to frightened children in a ruined chapel, and the woman beside me now, stronger, steadier, scarred and still standing. And I know this much: Sicily isn't the same. Neither are we. And that's a good thing. Because what we're building here? It's not what came before. It's better.

We leave the monastery at sunrise. Not because we're fleeing. Not this time. This time we walk without fear. The Germans are gone—fully withdrawn across the Strait of Messina, tail between their legs. The Allies have control now. Sicily is breathing again. Slowly, painfully, but it's breathing. Elena and I stand together at the gates as the villagers gather supplies. Maria loads blankets into the back of a cart. Mateo and Lucia sit side by side, eating bread and watching the road open in front of us. An Italian army truck pulls up—camouflage faded, but flying the right flag. Two young soldiers climb out and salute. "We've come to escort you back," one says. It still feels strange to hear good news spoken aloud. The road is rough but guarded. We walk with a convoy, two trucks of supplies, four Italian infantrymen, and twenty-five villagers who call Elena their guide and me their pilot, even though I haven't flown in days. No one talks much.

The weight of return is heavier than departure ever was. But it's a hopeful weight. There's no smoke on the horizon now. No snipers in the trees. Just spring beginning to stretch through the landscape, buds on the branches, distant birdsong, and the faint smell of salt from the sea. Elena walks beside me, a satchel across her shoulder and a rifle slung over her back. She doesn't look back once. Only forward. By midday, we crest the final ridge. And there it is. The village. What's left of it. Roofless houses. Crumbled walls. Burnt-out carts and torn-up ground. But somehow… it's still standing. The church bell lies cracked in the grass, but the steeple remains. The well is intact. The olive trees are blackened but alive. People begin to cry around us. Soft, stunned grief. But no one breaks down. Elena steps forward and drops to one knee. She presses her palm into the dirt, then closes her eyes. "We're home," she says.

The soldiers unload crates, food, medical supplies, tools. One of them finds an old tricolour Italian flag folded in his gear. He asks where to hang it. Elena points to the chapel.

"No crosses left," she says. "But a roof's a roof." He climbs the rafters and raises it slowly. When it catches the breeze and unfurls fully, everyone stops to watch. I don't think any of us breathe. It's not just a flag anymore. It's a promise. We spend the afternoon working. Clearing debris. Rebuilding doorframes. Fixing hinges with rusted nails and patience. Someone finds an old radio, dead, like ours, but we keep it. For the memory of the message that changed everything. At dusk, fires burn in the streets. Not from bombs. From cooking. The smell of soup drifts through the air. I sit on the church steps, polishing a dented mess tin, watching as children chase each other through alleyways I thought we'd never see again. Elena joins me.

Her dress is dusty, her arms scratched, and her smile, tired but real. "We lost so much," she says. I nod. "But we're still here." She looks up at the smoke curling into the sky. "I think this place can live again." I take her hand. "I think we can." And for once, we don't need words after that. We just sit there, hand in hand, beneath the sky we almost forgot how to look up at. Together. Finally.

By the second day back, we've opened the old bakery. It still smells faintly of soot, but the walls are standing. The oven works. Elena and two of the older women find flour in the supply crates and light the fire. Within hours, the scent of baking bread drifts through the broken alleys, and just like that—this place starts to feel like home again. Children run barefoot over cobblestones. The fountain flows once more. The churchyard, where we buried the first losses of the war, is cleared and planted with rosemary and basil. I don't know how we got here without breaking. But we did. And it's because of her. Elena hasn't stopped moving. She carries bundles of firewood from the chapel, teaches Mateo how to tie proper knots, oversees the rationing list with the calmness of someone who's done it under fire. The soldiers from the Italian unit respect her more than they do most of their own officers.

I catch her one evening standing in the doorway of the schoolhouse, staring into the half-rebuilt interior. Her arms are crossed. Her face unreadable. "What are you thinking?" I ask. She blinks, then turns. "That I don't know who I was before this. Before caves and flares and flight jackets. Before carrying half a village uphill in the rain." I move beside her, hands in my pockets. "You were someone strong. You just hadn't been tested yet." She smiles faintly. "And you?" "I was lost until I found you in that cave." She leans her shoulder into mine. "You found all of us." "No," I say. "You did." That night, we sleep under the stars again.

Not because we have to—but because we want to. The beds in the chapel are still being rebuilt, and no one minds a fire, a blanket, and a clear sky.

She lies beside me, head on my shoulder, the village quiet around us. The moonlight catches on the olive trees we once thought would never bear fruit again. "I can still hear the radio," she murmurs. "In my head." "So can I." Her hand finds mine in the dark. "We've got food. Safety. Children laughing again. But Jack..." Her voice falters. "Do you think it'll last?" I turn my head. I kiss her temple. "I don't know," I admit. "But I know this: if it doesn't, we'll fight again. And we'll win again. Because we've already lived through the worst." She exhales slowly, settles against me. And for a long time, we just lie there. Listening to the wind. Listening to the breath of something whole, something pure. And to the sound of a world that is, at last, quiet. Not silent. Just... at peace. We wake to birdsong. Not the shrill warning calls we learned to listen for during air raids—but real song. Bright, high, insistent. A string of notes that says, *"Get up. The war's over. There's work to do."* I stretch, groaning. Elena's head is still tucked against my chest, her hand resting over my heart like it belongs there. It does. She blinks slowly, then smiles. "Morning." I nod. "You hear that?" "The birds?" "Yeah." I grin. "I think they missed you."

By midmorning, the trucks roll in again. Allied supply crates. Italian engineers. A medic with a broken arm. Two civilians—one from Palermo, the other from Syracuse—looking for relatives. They've heard of a village that stood through the worst and kept its doors open. They mean our village. We help unload. Shovels. Seeds. Bed frames. Soap. Elena gives the young medic a slice of bread and thanks him for still showing up, arm in a sling and all. The new civilians stare at her like she's already mayor. Maybe she is. I spend the afternoon clearing what's left of the schoolhouse roof with Maria and three others. Hammer, nail, sun on our backs. The work is slow, but it's good. Real. Below, I hear Elena laughing. I lean over the broken frame and see her helping Lucia and Mateo draw chalk letters on the church steps—big, bold ones. **S-C-U-O-L-A.** School.

She claps for them when they finish. Mateo grins so wide his cheeks bunch under his eyes. The laughter echoes. And it stays. That night, the new arrivals join us at the fire. We pass cups of soup and whatever we can spare. One man sings an old folk tune about wheat fields. A woman plays a mouth harp. The children dance. Elena sits beside me. "They asked me if I would teach again," she says. "You said yes?" She nods. "I said I never really stopped." I raise my mug. "To you." "To us," she corrects, bumping her cup against mine. "You flew through fire and still came home." "Because you were here to come home to." We sit in the quiet when the music dies down. The fire burns low. The stars return. And Elena says something I didn't expect. "I want to plant olive trees." I look at her. "New ones?" "Yes. Not just to replace what was lost. To add something of our own. A sign that we didn't just survive. We grew."

I don't speak for a moment. Because I know what she's really saying. She's not going anywhere. Neither am I. "Then let's plant them," I say. "Together." She smiles, leans into me, and for the first time since the war began—since the cave, the flights, the monastery, the march—I let myself believe in something more than peace. I believe in life. And I believe in her. Tomorrow, we'll dig. We'll press our hands into the earth, together, and plant something that didn't exist before this war. Something green and patient. Something that needs time and tenderness and weather, the way we once did. Not to forget what we have lost. But to remember and honour those that have fought for our freedom here in Sicily.

To let it take root in something quieter, something kinder. These trees that we will plant, they will not grow overnight.

Beneath a Sky of Hope

It will take many seasons. Years. They'll bend under wind. They'll crack in drought. But they'll hold. Like we did. And maybe, long after we're gone, someone will sit beneath their branches and feel something they can't name. A trace of survival. A whisper of love.

I look at her now, Elena, her profile lit by firelight and stars, eyes soft, hands steady. I wonder if she knows what she is to me. What she's always been. A map through darkness. A voice in silence. The reason I came home in the first place. I reach for her hand, and she gives it easily, like it's always belonged there. The wind moves through the olive trees behind us, low and warm and ancient. And in that moment, beneath the hush of a Sicilian sky stitched with stars, I know something I'll never forget: We are not just survivors. We are roots and bloom. We are the story after the storm. We are the beginning of what comes next— And what comes next is ours.

Ana Monroy

17

A Quiet Proposal

The next morning, the horizon is the colour of honey and smoke. A gentle breeze stirs the ash-thin dust rising from the square where we'll plant the first olive tree. Mateo carries a spade almost too big for his shoulders. Elena follows him with a bundle of saplings cradled like something sacred. I should feel settled. Rooted. But something inside me won't let go of the thought I've been turning over in my mind for days. I've tried to leave it alone. I can't anymore. After the tree is in the ground—after the villagers clap and Elena wipes her brow with the back of her wrist and smiles at the soil like it's answered a prayer, I take her aside.

We walk along the path beyond the well, past the last stone archway, until the village disappears behind us. The hills stretch on, soft and gold, not a trace of war in sight. Just wild thyme and olive branches catching sunlight. "Elena," I say, my voice a little rougher than I mean it to be. She glances at me, curious. "What is it?" I stop walking. So does she. The silence between us hums with everything I haven't said. "I want you to come to England with me." Her brow knits, but she doesn't look away. "England?" "To Long-parish. Hampshire. It's where my parents live. My home. Or... the closest thing to it." She says nothing. "I've written them," I continue, filling the quiet. "Told them about Sicily. About what we've been through. About you." Her eyes flicker at that. "They want to meet you. And I—I want you to see where I come from. I want to give you something... quiet.

Not temporary. A breath that isn't borrowed from survival." Still no answer. So, I try again. "You've given everything to this place. But I think you deserve to see a world that isn't always rebuilding itself from rubble. Just for a little while. Come with me. Let's leave Sicily—for a season, not forever. Let's find out what peace looks like somewhere green, somewhere safe." She looks past me then, to the horizon. The sky is clear.

The light on her face is soft, thoughtful. "You'd take me there?" she asks quietly. "Even now, when things are still fragile?" "I'd take you anywhere," I say. "But I want this for you. For us." She doesn't smile yet. She just takes my hand. And squeezes. She doesn't speak right away. Just stands there, hand in mine, her eyes tracing the distant folds of the hills like she's trying to draw courage from their shape. "I haven't left Sicily in my entire life," she says finally. I nod. "I know." "My parents are buried here. My childhood. Every memory that made me who I am." "You wouldn't be leaving it behind," I say gently. "You'd be carrying it forward."

Her lips press together. "And the village?" "They'll be okay. They've learned how to live again. Because of you. They'll keep going." She looks at me now. Really looks. Her gaze searches mine like she's weighing what I'm offering against the quiet sense of duty she's worn like skin since this war began. Then she exhales—slow, deep. "I don't know how to be anywhere else." "You don't have to know yet," I say. "You just have to be willing to find out." Her eyes begin to glisten, not from fear, I think, but from the sheer weight of change. From the idea that something new might finally be allowed.

I cup her face gently, my thumbs brushing the curve of her cheek. "Elena... I love you. And I want to show you the places that built me, the people who raised me. I want you to know where I came from, just like I know what you've survived. Let's give ourselves something unburned. Something whole." She swallows. "Longparish," she says, testing the word on her tongue like it's foreign and familiar all at once. "Hampshire. What's it like?" "Quiet. Rolling green fields. Cold streams. Tea that doesn't taste like mud."

I smile, coaxing a flicker of a laugh from her. "And a garden with wildflowers my mother never quite gets under control." She steps into my arms, folding against my chest, the way she does when words are too small for what she feels. "I think I want to go," she whispers. "With you." The wind tugs at her skirt. Olive branches rustle behind us. I hold her tighter. "Then we'll go. Together." Back in the village, no one asks questions when we start preparing to leave. Maria presses dried herbs into Elena's hands. Lucia draws us a picture of the chapel with two olive trees and a yellow sun. Mateo tries to act brave, but he hugs me so hard I have to kneel. That night, the church bell rings once—just once—as if to bless our departure. We don't take much. Just what fits in a pack. A photograph. A letter. A folded ribbon. Memories pressed between the pages of a worn book. But we carry everything that matters. And when the road opens the next morning, when the transport rolls in, when I take Elena's hand as we step up onto the truck that will lead us to the sea, I know one thing for certain: We are not escaping Sicily. We are walking toward something new. Together.

Elena doesn't cry when we leave Sicily. She watches the coast shrink behind us from the back of the military truck—her spine straight, her hands folded in her lap, her chin lifted like she refuses to let the land see her falter. Like she's saying goodbye to the bones of her childhood without letting them bury her in return. We don't speak much on the road to Palermo. The truck rattles over gravel and silence. I glance at her sometimes, wanting to say something that might soften the ache of departure—but I don't need to. Her eyes say enough. They carry the village, the monastery, the olive trees, the war. All of it. Every life she helped save, every loss she's still learning to live with. She carries it not like a burden, but like a vow. And still, she moves forward.

The ferry to mainland Italy is crowded with soldiers, aid workers, and a handful of civilians. Elena sits at the edge of the upper deck, wind tugging at the loose strands of her hair. She stares at the water like she's trying to teach herself what freedom feels like. When I sit beside her, she doesn't look away. "This is harder than I thought," she says softly. "Leaving." I nod. "You're not alone in that." "It's not just home," she adds. "It's... the version of me that only ever knew how to survive." I look at her—really look—and in this moment, I don't see the girl from the chapel or the woman pulling bandages from an Allied crate. I see someone stepping into the unknown with nothing, but courage and history braided into her soul. "You don't have to leave her behind," I say. "She can come too. But you don't owe her the rest of your life." Elena's eyes meet mine. Brighter now. Still solemn, still deep. But no longer clenched around fear. "I want to meet the version of me who isn't waiting for the next disaster," she whispers. I take her hand. "Then we'll find her. Together."

We pass through Naples, then north to Rome, then across

the Channel on a fog-thick morning that smells of salt and coal smoke. She clutches her coat tighter. Everything feels foreign, no olive trees, no cracked sun-dried walls. Just green fields and grey skies that stretch on like pages yet to be written. When the train slows through Hampshire, Elena leans into me and whispers: "This is your Sicily." And I smile. Because she's right. Because this, this quiet, mossy country—isn't just where I came from. It's where she might finally rest. The train slows as we roll into Longparish. It is green all over it blankets the land in a way I forgot was possible. Everything is soft here, hedgerows stitched like patchwork, narrow lanes curled between trees, and cottages with moss on their roofs like they've always belonged to the earth. Elena presses a hand to the window glass. Her breath fogs the pane. "It doesn't even look real," she murmurs. "It is," I say gently. "And now it's yours too."

She doesn't answer right away. Just keeps staring out like she's cataloguing the quiet, unsure if she's allowed to trust it. My parents wait at the station—my mother in her good coat, holding a wool scarf she clearly knit for the occasion, and my father trying not to pace. When we step off the train, Elena stays close, her fingers brushing mine like a tether. I introduce them slowly. "This is Elena," I say. My mother takes her hand first, both palms warm and sure. "We're so grateful you're here, my dear." My father nods. "Welcome home." Elena blinks once, then nods, her lips parting slightly like she might cry, but she doesn't. She just smiles, soft and stunned. I see it happen in that moment; something shifts inside her. The space between fear and peace begins to close.

We walk to the house. A narrow stone cottage wrapped in ivy and quiet. The garden gate creaks. A blackbird scurries through the hedges. My mother's tea roses bloom despite the chill. Elena stops in the doorway. I almost ask if she's alright, but she speaks before I can. "This reminds me of a storybook I read as a child." "Good," I whisper. "You deserve to live one."

Inside, she runs her fingers across the bookshelf, the hearth, the wooden beams as if memorising the texture of this new life. It's not grand. It's not even large. But it's whole. And when she sees the window facing the field, her voice barely makes a sound. "It's beautiful." "You're safe here," I say. She nods once. Then leans her head against my shoulder and whispers: "I can breathe." The fire crackles low in the sitting room. The air smells faintly of rosemary and ash, and somewhere in the kitchen, my mother is humming, the same tune she always hums when the stew is ready.

Elena stands at the window, watching dusk stretch its long limbs across the field. The light here is different than Sicily — softer, paler, touched with mist instead of dust. She looks like she belongs here already, even if she doesn't believe it yet. "Dinner's ready," I say. She turns, blinking as if I've pulled her from a dream. But she smiles. And that's all I need. We sit around the oak table beneath the low beams, candles flickering between the bread and bowls.

My father says grace, and though Elena bows her head, I can tell she's watching everything, taking it all in like it's a language she hasn't spoken in years but still remembers somewhere deep. My mother passes the stew. "Not Sicilian, I'm afraid." Elena laughs, quiet, genuine. "It smells better than half of what we made during the war." "You'll have to teach me one day," my mother says. "I'd like that," Elena replies. And she means it. The conversation is slow, easy. No pressure. Just questions gently offered like gifts. My father asks about the olive trees. My mother asks about the children in the village.

Elena answers in pieces at first, short sentences, long pauses. But then, slowly, her voice begins to stretch into stories. She tells them about Maria and Lucia, about the cave where they lit candles against fear. She describes the bell in the monastery, the way the wind sounded the morning the Germans finally left. She speaks about the radio. And the message. And when she falters, when her hand tightens around her spoon, my mother reaches across and touches her wrist, eyes soft with understanding. "You're safe now, Elena," she says. And I watch something unspoken pass between them. A thread. A permission. Elena nods. "I'm starting to believe it." After dinner, we sit in the quiet. Outside, the stars come out, faint behind wisps of fog, but there. My father brings out a bottle of elderflower cordial. My mother begins knitting again, listening as Elena talks softly about the orchard she hopes to plant when she returns. And I sit beside her, my arm brushing hers, the fire warming the room, the past gently stepping back to let something else take its place. For the first time in years, I see Elena at rest. Not surviving. Just... being.

Later, when we climb the stairs to the guest room, she stands by the window, looking out into the moonlit garden. "I never imagined anything like this," she says. I come up behind her, wrapping my arms around her waist. "Like what?" "This kind of quiet. This kind of home." I kiss the side of her neck, just below her ear. "You deserve all of it." She turns to face me, fingers brushing my jaw. "I think I want to stay. Just for a while." I nod. "Then we'll stay." And as she pulls me into her arms, I know that this, this room, this night, this soft beginning, is no longer just a pause between storms. It's the start of something real.

The morning is crisp, the kind that bites at your cheeks just enough to feel alive. Mist clings low over the fields, curling through the hedgerows like a ghost reluctant to leave. Birds stir in the branches above, and the ground beneath our boots is soft with dew. Elena walks beside me, her scarf knotted loosely, hair braided back.

She doesn't speak at first, but her gaze is everywhere, the low stone fences, the sheep in the pasture, the copper leaves clinging stubbornly to late autumn branches. "I never imagined England would be so... gentle," she says finally. I glance at her. "Gentle's not the word I'd use for it growing up. But maybe it is now." She smiles faintly. "Maybe we're different now. Maybe it takes surviving a storm to notice calm when it finally arrives." We walk a while without speaking. The quiet here isn't like Sicily's. It's heavier, padded with soil and fog and history instead of sun and wind. But it's still peace. And we know the weight of both.

We reach the edge of the field where the stream runs slow

beneath an old wooden bridge. I step up first and turn to help her across, but she pauses halfway. "What is it?" I ask. She looks down into the water, the reflection of her face distorted in the ripples. "Do you ever think we're living someone else's life?"

I shake my head. "No. I think we've earned this one." She lifts her eyes to mine. "I want to believe that." "You can." I take her hands, and for a long breath, we stand still, surrounded by mist and birdsong and the low, distant toll of the village bell — not a warning anymore. Just the hour. A soft hour. Ours. She steps off the bridge, into the field, her boots damp with frost, her eyes wide with something that looks like beginning. "What would we do if we stayed here longer?" she asks, almost shyly. "What does life look like… after all that?" I catch up to her, threading my fingers through hers. "Well,"

I say, "There's a market on Saturdays. A neighbour down the lane who always needs help with lambing season. A meadow that floods every spring and leaves wild poppies in its wake." She smiles. "Poppies." "We could plant a garden," I add. "Apples. Courgettes. Maybe a greenhouse if we're ambitious." "And olive trees?" I laugh. "They don't grow here, you know." She lifts a brow. "We'll teach them."

We both laugh then, the kind that starts small and blooms from the chest like something healing.

As the sun lifts higher, we turn back toward the house. Smoke curls from the chimney. A robin darts across the sky. Elena rests her head against my shoulder. Her voice is quieter now, but sure. "I could see myself here. With you." "Then stay," I say. "Let's make something that doesn't need to be fixed. Let's build something new." And as we walk home, step by step, through a world that no longer asks us to run, I realise something I've never let myself believe until now: This is not the end of the road. It's the beginning of our own. I find her at the kitchen table, just after lunch, the sunlight pouring through the leaded windows, softening everything it touches. There's a half-empty mug of tea beside her, long gone cold. A small inkwell. Paper the colour of old lace. She doesn't hear me at first.

She is deep in thought, pen pressed gently to the page, her head tilted in that quiet way she does when she's writing something that matters. Her face is still, but her eyes flicker, remembering. I don't speak. I just watch. Because this — this — is the Elena I love most. The one who carries the whole world inside her. She finishes writing and sets the pen down, sighing softly. Only then does she notice me. "Sorry," she says with a small smile. "I didn't hear you." "That's alright," I reply, crossing the room. "Is that a letter?" She nods. "To Maria."

I pull out the chair beside her and sit. "May I?" She hesitates, then slides the paper toward me. "Just… don't judge my handwriting." I take the page carefully. Her script is neat, deliberate, each word weighted like it was chosen more than once.

I read:

Dearest Maria,

England is not what I imagined. It is softer. Quieter. Like waking up inside a different kind of dream. There are green hills, Jack's mother makes tea with honey, and the sky is full of birds that don't scatter when you walk by. I'm still learning how to live without listening for engines overhead. But I think I'm healing. Slowly. And I think it's alright that it's slow. Tell Lucia that the roses here bloom even when it's cold. Tell Mateo that I haven't forgotten how to plant things. Tell them I miss them. But tell them this, too: Peace feels real   now.
And I'm not afraid to build something here. Love always, Elena

I set the page down. I don't speak right away. She looks at

me carefully. "Too much?" "No," I whisper. "It's perfect." That evening, we walk to the post-box at the end of the lane. Elena slips the envelope in slowly, almost reverently, then lets it go. "That was a piece of you," I say as we turn back. She nods. "It was also a choice." "Of what?" "To live again." I take her hand in mine. "I think," she says softly, "I want to stay. Not just visit. I want to build something here with you." My heart knocks once, hard. And in that quiet moment, between leaf-shadow and lamplight, I know that this woman—this warrior, survivor, teacher, healer, has chosen me as the place she wants to rest. And I will spend the rest of my days making sure she never forgets that she deserves to bloom, not just survive.

18

Ana Monroy

A Thread Across the Sea

The English morning sun has already warmed the garden wall by the time Elena hears the soft knock at the door. She is kneeling beside the rosemary bed, her hands deep in the soil, sleeves dusted in earth. I am chopping firewood just beyond the shed, my axe rising and falling in a steady rhythm. She wipes her palms on her skirt and stands tall. The knock came again, tentative, polite. When she opens the door, there is no one standing there. Just a bicycle propped against the gate and a small envelope tucked into the corner of the sill, weighed down by a polished river stone. Elena picks it up carefully. The return address makes her heart catch. **Sicily.** She does not open it at once. Instead, she carries it to the back of the house, and she sits beneath the pear tree, tracing her fingers over the handwriting on the front. Maria. It was unmistakable. Bold and looping. Slightly too large, like the words wanted more space than the paper allowed.

Elena holds the envelope for a while longer, then slips her

fingers under the edge and opens it. Inside, three things: a folded letter, a pressed sprig of thyme, and a small drawing, a child's sketch of a tree with wide roots, a girl beneath it, arms outstretched. Lucia's drawing. Her throat tightened. She unfolded the letter.

Dearest Elena,

The village misses your steps. The church feels different without your voice, though Maria insists you're still echoing in the stone. We are well — or as well as people can be who have learned to live again. The Germans are gone, truly gone now. Italian soldiers have returned, and the children play in the square again. Lucia teaches the younger ones your songs. Mateo insists he will become a gardener like you and Jack, though he says England must be very cold for olive trees. We heard from the soldiers that you are safe. That you have peace. That you are with someone who looks at you like you're a light in the dark. I hope it's true. We will always miss you, but we are not afraid for you. Because you have become something more than our Elena. You are someone the world needs whole. Stay, if it's right. Grow where you are planted. And if the wind ever carries you home again, we'll be waiting. Con amore, Maria.

Elena closes her eyes as Maria's words eased her guilt and longing; she realizes she does not have to choose between her two homes. One shaped her, while the other gave her room to grow. She folds the letter, touches the thyme to her lips, and walks into the sunlight-filled kitchen.

That afternoon, Elena is alone outside she walks behind the cottage, the hills quiet and a light breeze blows against her long flowing hair, Maria's letter is tucked secretly in her cardigan pocket. The sun moves lazily across the sky, soft and gold, warm even in late autumn. She breaths in the scent of cut grass, and in the distant there is chimney smoke, and the sharp freshness of cold soil. As she walks, she lets herself wonder. Not just about what has been. But about what could be. She arrives at the old oak tree I once described from Sicily, sits beneath it, and opens her notebook. The page is blank. But her hands do not tremble. She begins to write. Not a letter. Not a diary. A plan.

A garden with space for herbs and small children's feet. A table where others might sit and eat and feel safe. A classroom, maybe just a room in the village hall, where she could teach again, not out of necessity, but out of joy. Bookshelves. A window that faced the rising sun. A home where no one had to whisper anymore.

She studies the list, then adds: *A life made of choosing, not surviving.* Back at the cottage, she finds me in the garden, hands in compost and wind-tousled hair. I look up with a boyish grin as she approaches.

"Find anything?" I ask. Elena lifts her notebook. "Just the rest of my life." I wipe my hands. "Can I read it?" She shakes her head. "Not yet." She hugs me, resting her head on my chest. My heartbeat responds. "I want to build something here," she says softly. "I want roots." I kiss her forehead. "Let's plant them." The light was fading by the time we went inside. A fire crackles softly in the hearth, and dinner is simmering on the stove. Elena stands by the window as night falls; her hand is resting lightly on the sill. Tomorrow would come. Quietly, softly, with frost on the roof and birdsong in the hedgerows. But tonight, tonight she knows, without fear, that she is no longer waiting to be rescued from her life. She is living it. Fully. Freely. And she is ready for whatever comes next. It began with a notice in the corner shop. A handwritten card, slightly askew on the corkboard near the milk crates:

"Seeking help with village children's reading hour — Tuesdays, 3:30 afternoon, church hall."

Elena stares at it for a long time, her hand still resting on the bag of flour she has come in for. Somehow, it felt as though it had been waiting for her. She takes the card down and slips it into her coat pocket. That afternoon, she walks the rugged mile into the village, her boots crunching over damp leaves, the air fills with woodsmoke and distant birdsong. The church hall I had previously mentioned is situated at a considerable distance; its red brick exterior, small windows, and ivy-covered walls evoke a sense of enduring memory. Inside, the air smells of wood, chalk, and paper. Elena greets the vicar's wife, who welcomes her and gestures to a stack of books. "We have about a dozen, some unusual. They'll enjoy meeting you." Elena smiles, her heart is quickening with anticipation.

The children arrive, noisy and messy, their chatter echoing through the hall and pencils tapping on tabletops. Henry shows Elena a drawing, the crayon lines bold and earnest; Grace hands her a portrait—Elena's smile captured in quick, affectionate strokes. They read stories aloud, Elena's voice is weaving through the room, there is shared memories of Sicily—olive trees shimmering in the night air, the lull of distant waves under starlit skies, the rise of song during storms that rattled old shutters. The smell of chalk dust mingles with the sweetness of children's hair, and laughter spilled from every corner, so that when the hour ends, no one, not even Elena, is eager to leave.

After the laughter fades and the children departed, a gentle quiet settled over her, lingering as she returns to the cottage. The crackle of the fire mingles with the faint scent of damp earth from her boots, while the wind rattles softly against the windowpanes. She sits beside the hearth, boots drying near the warmth, her fingers tingling from the cold and the memory of small hands pressed into hers. I hand Elena a mug of tea and kiss her cheek. Steam curls from the cup, carrying the scent of chamomile and honey. "You smell like chalk and children," I said warmly. Elena smiles, her hands curl around the cup, feeling the heat seep into her skin. "I think I might love it," she murmured, her voice soft with contentment. I watch at her then eyes gentle, thoughtful, soaking in the peace that seemed to settle around her shoulders. "You're building something here," I said at last. She nods, turning to look at me, her expression open and quietly luminous. "So are you," she whispers. For a long moment, we simply sit together, letting the warmth and quiet wrap around us, two young souls who have spent years running, now learning, at last, how to stay.

It arrived on a Thursday: a pale blue envelope, the corners are bent and soft as though it has travelled tucked against the warmth of other letters. Her name appears in Lucia's careful script, the loops familiar and gentle, the ink smudged ever so slightly near the edge. The envelope is cool to the touch, its paper grainy beneath Elena's fingertips, carrying a faint scent of orange blossom—sunlit, distant, achingly sweet. It rests among the usual post: a delivery schedule, a seed catalogue, and a scribbled reminder from the village shop about the firewood she still hasn't collected. But it was Lucia's handwriting that caught her first, the shape of the letters making Elena's heart skip, just once, sharp and bright, before settling into a quiet ache of longing. She paused, memory tugging her back to the last letter from Sicily, the way she'd lingered over each word, the sense of home held between paper and ink. For a moment, Elena simply holds the envelope, breathing in the promise of distant voices and stories brought across the miles, before she slowly turns it over in her hands, anticipation fluttering in her chest.

She carries it to the garden and sits beneath the pear tree, now bare of leaves but still strong. The earth around it is damp and cold, and a soft mist curls along the edge of the field. Her hands tremble with anticipation, memories of distant shores pressing at her heart. She does not open the letter right away. She holds onto it. Felling the weight of the sea between the pages. And then, gently, she unfolded it.

Ciao Elena, Maria helped me write this. She says my spelling is still a disaster, but I told her you wouldn't mind. I miss you. Mateo misses you too. He says you would like the new puppy that lives behind the chapel. We named her Luna. The olive tree you planted is growing. I water it like you taught me. I told the tree a story yesterday, just like you used to do. I think it liked it. It's leaning toward the sun more now. Sometimes I look up at the sky and wonder what your new sky looks like. I hope it's soft. Maria says you are building a new life. That you are still singing, even if we can't hear you. That makes me feel better. I told the younger ones that you're not gone. You're just growing in a different direction.
Love,
Lucia

Elena folds the letter and presses it to her chest, feeling the gentle weight of the paper against her heart, the coolness of its grain warming beneath her touch. As she does, memories of the olive tree unfurl, sunlit leaves shimmering, the scent of earth and olives carried on the Sicilian breeze. The story within the letter seems to travel through her, whispering softly into the roots of the tree she once tended, binding present tenderness to the deep soil of her past.

And she weeps, not from grief, but from love. A love that had stretched itself across distance and time and still found its way home. Later, she tucked Lucia's letter between the pages of her notebook. That evening, she reads it aloud to me beneath the kitchen lamplight. I listen without interrupting, just holding her hand as her voice softens with emotions. "She says I'm growing in a different direction," Elena murmurs, brushing a tear from her cheek. "You are," he replied. "And they see it. They understand." Elena smiled. "Maybe that's what love is, too. Letting someone change." "Or helping them bloom," I said.

As the night deepens and wind curls around the corners of the cottage, Elena, in her mind, conjures scenes of Sicily. She could almost smell the sweet tang of lemons drifting from Maria's Garden and hear Luna's playful bark echoing through sunlit groves; the olive tree, leaves trembling, leaning towards the warmth of the sun. The cool stone beneath her palms, the earthy scent of tilled soil, and the distant call of nightjars filling her senses. A gentle ache lingers for what was lost, but it fades into warmth as Elena recognizes how each memory had shaped her new life. And she knows, deeply, gently, that she has not left anything behind. She had simply brought it forward, into this new life, this love, this new sky.

The invitation came in the form of a gentle knock at the door. It was Margaret, the vicar's wife, standing beneath the low eaves in her wool coat and wellington boots, cheeks pink with wind. She smiles as Elena opens the door. "The village is holding a winter gathering," she murmurs. "A quiet one. Nothing grand. Just stories and songs, a bit of food and warmth." Elena takes the small paper, fingers brushing its neat edges. Her name is inked on it. Printed gently among the others. A pause. Margaret insists, "We were wondering if you might share something. About Sicily. About the children. Anything you'd like." Elena blinked. "Me?" "You've become part of this place," Margaret said, her voice kind. "You see your story… it's already taking root in our hearts and branching out through all of us. We find ourselves changed by every word you share, it is as if your journey has given us new leaves to grow from." The village hall was full of candlelight and soft chatter. Tables of jam jars and knitted scarves lined the walls, and children darted between benches with mittens swinging from their sleeves. Elena stands near the back at first, unsure. My hand found hers beneath the folds of her shawl.

I reached out, my hand resting gently atop of hers, and I offer quietly, "You don't have to speak if you don't want to." As the words settled in the quiet, I watch her face for any flicker of tension, acutely aware of how heavy silence could be. I long for her to know that her comfort mattered more than any answer, that sometimes presence speaks louder than conversation. In that moment, I hope she could sense I was not just to there to listen, but to simply be with her, no matter what she chooses. But she does. Not because she needs to prove anything. But because something in her heart has shifted. When her name is called, she gradually walks to the front slowly. The murmurs fade. Firelight flickers behind her, warming her spine. She has no notes, doesn't carry a script.

She simply begins. "I used to believe that survival meant silence," she said softly. "That if I kept my head down, kept others safe, it didn't matter if I was seen." She looks out at them, faces unfamiliar and familiar, farmers and schoolteachers, children who'd sat at her feet on Tuesdays. "But there's a kind of living that's louder than survival," she said. "It's in planting seeds. It's in reading stories aloud. It's in standing in a room like this and knowing no one expects you to disappear." A hush settles over the room, tender and whole. "In Sicily, we sang when we were afraid. Here, I've learned to sing without fear." She pauses, searching for the last line not in memory, but in truth. "And that… is its own kind of freedom."

She, Elena, sits back down beside me, and I take her hand, lacing our fingers together. "They love you," I whisper. Elena smiles faintly, still breathless from the quiet release that comes with speaking the truth aloud. "They see me," she says. And this time, her words feel less like a discovery and more like a homecoming. Outside, the snow falls softly, not in sheets or storms, but in a drifting hush, pale flakes tumbling like tiny letters from the sky. By morning, the garden is dusted in white, the field a wide, untouched sheet of parchment. Elena stands at the window, a steaming mug in her hands, watching a robin hop through the frost.

Behind her, the hearth set in front of the fireplace crackles and breathes warmth into the room. Somewhere in the cottage, she could hear me moving about earlier, humming low under my breath, the old kettle clanking as I fill it from the pump outside. The scent of woodsmoke lingers inside meanwhile, mingling with the sharp chill that creeps in from beneath the door. Outside, the pear tree stood in its winter skin, still, waiting, rooted. So much like the both of us. After we share a quiet morning together, we step outside. The cold is present in a soft rush, and each step crunches gently in the snow, the silence between us is tender and unhurried. We walk after breakfast, down the lane, past the village where the bell has not rung in warning for months, and across the edge of the wood where holly bushes shimmer red against the white. I do not say much, letting the quiet landscape fill the space between us, each breath drawing in the crisp air and the faint tang of smoke, grounding us in the steady rhythm of our shared morning.

My hand glove stays folded in hers. Easy. Sure. The way it always has. As we reach the clearing near the old oak, Elena pauses. She looks up at the branches, bare and reaching. "I never thought peace would feel like this," she said softly. I look at her, snow caught in the edges of his hair, my eyes steady. "Like what?" "Not loud. Not grand. Just… simple." I nodded. "Like breathing." She smiled. "Like growing." I step closer, hands still in my coat pockets. "There's something I want to ask you." Elena tilts her head. "Now?" My smile was small, nervous in the way that made her love me more. "I've been waiting for the right moment." "And this is it?" I glance around, at the snow, the stillness, a single robin perches on a branch above us. "It feels like one." Then, with that same quiet grace that had always defined me, I reach into my pocket and pull out a small wooden box worn at the corners. I open it. Inside it is a golden ring. A thin band with a curve that caught the light like the arc of a rising moon.

"I don't need a ceremony," I softly gesture. "I don't need a crowd." I take her hand. Her fingers trembling slightly in mine, warm and uncertain, anchoring me in the quiet hush of snowfall. "I just need you. For as long as we're both still growing." Elena didn't speak right away. She looked at the ring. Then at me. A glimmer of uncertainty flickering in her eyes, quickly softened by a quiet hope as she let herself breathe into the moment, her thumb tracing the edge of the golden band. And somewhere in her chest, the place that had once been filled with war and shadows, something settled. Not like an ending. But like a beginning. "Yes," she whispered. "Of course, yes." I sigh with relief, and my face lights up like sunlight through fog. I slip the ring on her finger. It fits like it had always been there. We stand together in the snow, not in triumph, not in rescue, but in peace. In love that has been earned, quietly, day by day. Not a single moment has been simple, but this one was. Elena presses her forehead to mine. "I was never waiting to be saved," she said. I nodded. "I know." I smile. "But I was always meant to be found." The pear tree had begun to bear fruit. Small at first, hard as stone and shy of the sun. But they grew. Day by day. And now, just past midsummer, the branches hung low with promise. Elena kneels in the grass beneath it, a wide-brimmed hat shading her eyes as she reaches up and gently pressing her fingers to the fruit's smooth skin. It gave slightly under her touch.

The house emanates subtle sounds in the background. I navigate the kitchen, opening the window with a quiet creak and attend to the softly whistling kettle. The air holds the aroma of herbs and freshly baked bread. She places her hand on the earth, which now retains the memory of her presence, the impression of her kneeling, her footsteps, and the rhythm of her planting are evident. The morning mail contains two letters from Sicily: one from Maria and another, in a floral envelope, unmistakably from Lucia. Elena opens both methodically, approaching the correspondence with composure. Lucia has enclosed a new drawing depicting their former cave illuminated by yellow candles, accompanied by an illustration of Elena, portrayed amidst a garden of sunflowers.

Elena runs her thumb along the rough, slightly smudged edge of Lucia's drawing, feeling the grooves where the pencil pressed hardest and tracing the sunflowers blooming in the candlelit cave. Golden afternoon light spills over the table, catching on the paper and painting the room in a gentle glow. There are no aches behind her ribs anymore. Just warmth, like the comfort of a well-tended fire on a winter's night. She remembers the days when just looking at drawings from home made her chest tighten, the ache of loss and longing sharp as frost. Now, all that remains is softness, a sense that each memory, once heavy with sorrow, has been transformed into the gentle heat of belonging.

She places the letter in her journal by the door, filled with memories and dreams. That afternoon, she meets Margaret at the hall, where children are waiting with books and pencils. Bea, about seven, greets Elena excitedly and offers her a purple crayon. They spend the hour reading, drawing, and learning together. Calm and steady, Elena guides them, feeling trusted and appreciated as their laughter fills the room.

On the walk home, the sun cast a golden veil over the hills, and the air buzzed with bees in the hedgerows. I meet her at the garden gate, holding a basket of new vegetables. "I thought you'd want to pick the first pear," I said. We stand beneath the tree as she reaches up and twists the ripest fruit gently from the branch. It comes loose with a soft snap. Elena turns it over in her hand, the skin a pale green blush, the weight firm and real. She takes a bite. Sweet, clean, grounded.

I watch her. "So?" She nods slowly, smiling with her whole face. "It tastes like home." That night, after dinner, we sit on the bench beneath the tree, the sky darkening with stars above them, the warm hush of evening curling around our shoulders like a second blanket. Elena leans into me, my hand resting gently on her knee. "I used to think survival meant endurance," she said quietly. "That if I just kept going, kept holding everything together, I was living." I didn't interrupt. "But this," she continues, her voice soft but sure, "This is living. This garden. These letters. You." I looked down at her, the edge of a smile tugging at my mouth. "I hope it never feels like a cage." She shakes her head. "No. It feels like air." And as the wind brushes gently on the leaves above us the stars twinkle in the night sky. Elena closes her eyes, for the first time in her life, letting go of every weight that didn't belong to her anymore. She was no longer waiting for a life to begin. She was already in it.

Beneath a Sky of Hope

Ana Monroy

19

When The Light Finds Her

Today, the church bells ring just once, low, soft, like they don't want to interrupt the stillness of the morning. I'm standing at the edge of the garden, my hands are tucked into the pockets of my jacket, watching as the sunlight threads itself through the trees and spills golden hues across the grass. The old pear tree behind the cottage is in full bloom, Elena says it waits for the right time. I know what she means. Everything in my life began the moment she stepped out of the village and into the cave in Sicily with me. I can recollect the children gathering around her and the world falling apart around us. Everything thereafter was a fight for survival. The villagers coming with us and keeping us uplifted. Of course we did.

Margaret and the vicar are holding hands. Little Bea is

clutching a huge bouquet. Maria couldn't travel today, her letter arrived two days ago, folded with care, tied in a red thread, and tucked into the pages of Elena's wedding book like a blessing. My parents have been weeping quietly all morning. Mother pretends she is not crying over Elena's hand-stitched veil, but I see her wipe her cheek twice while pretending to arrange wildflowers. There's no grand aisle. No orchestra. Just a path cut through the tall grass and chairs set beneath the archway we built together, wood carved with stars and olive branches. And now she's walking toward me. She wears white, simple, linen, a ribbon at her waist. Her hair is pinned back with soft curls brushing her shoulders. In her hands is a small bouquet of rosemary, thyme, and one flower I do not recognise but know must be Sicilian. She walks slowly. Steady. Like she's not just walking toward me, but toward a life she chooses. And I... I forget to breathe. Because there's something about seeing her like this, her eyes calm, her shoulders light, that makes every moment of war and loss and waiting worth it.

This is the woman I fell in love with when the world was crumbling. And this is the woman I will love now that we're building something new. We speak our vows beneath the trees. No paper. No rehearsal. Just the words we've carried inside us for months. "I choose you," I say, "not because I need saving or because you do. But because I want to wake beside you every morning and know we're still here. Still choosing." Her voice is steady when she replies. "And I choose you," she says. "Because even when I had nothing, you never made me feel like I was less. And now that I have everything, it still starts and ends with you." She slides the ring onto my hand. I slip hers onto her finger — the same one I gave her under falling snow a year ago. We kiss. And the world is quiet — not out of reverence, but because it knows there's nothing else left to say.

That night, we sit beneath the pear tree — husband and wife. The candlelight from the tables still flickers in the distance, laughter drifting from the hall where the music hasn't quite stopped. But here, beneath the stars, it's just us. Elena leans into my chest, her hand tucked in mine. "We're married," she whispers, smiling. "We are." "And tomorrow?" "We'll dig," I tell her, repeating the words she once said to me in a cave full of shadows. "We'll plant. We'll live." And she closes her eyes, rests her head against me, and says the one thing that undoes me completely. "I'm not afraid anymore." The stars glow above us. The garden breathes. And in her arms, I know the truth I never dared hope for during the years I spent in flight, in war, in silence: Love is not a miracle. It is a decision made every morning. And she, this woman, my wife, is the most beautiful decision I will ever make.

The stars deepen above us, and the air cools, but neither of us moves. She stays curled into me beneath the pear tree, the layers of her dress gathered in her lap, her bare feet brushing against mine. Somewhere beyond the hedge, I can still hear the gentle rhythm of music from the hall, a fiddle, a piano, laughter. But here, in our small circle of candlelight and earth, time has slowed. Elena shifts, tilting her head up to look at me. The glow from the lantern catches the edges of her face — her eyes soft, lashes long, her lips parted like she's about to tell me a secret. "What is it?" I ask. She shakes her head lightly. "Nothing." "Tell me." She hesitates, then presses her hand against my chest. "Do you ever feel like it's too good to be real?" I don't rush to answer. I hold her gaze, and I think about all the days I thought I wouldn't live to see this. All the nights I imagined her in darkness, surrounded by fear and children who only knew war. And now… she's here. We are here. "Every single day," I say. "But I also know this is the only thing that ever felt real." She exhales, like something she didn't know she was holding loosens in her chest. "Good," she whispers. "Then I'm not alone in it."

I stand and offer my hand. She rises gracefully, barefoot in the grass, dress floating around her like breath. I lead her into the cottage, past the kitchen where the last of the cake waits on the counter and the jar of rosemary is still open beside the sink. The fire is still warm in the hearth. I light a single candle and place it on the table. She walks slowly through the room, trailing her fingers over the worn edge of the table, the carved mantlepiece, the window ledge where she once wrote dreams in a notebook by moonlight. "This place," she says quietly, turning to me. "It's ours now." I walk toward her. "It always was." She meets me halfway, and when I kiss her when she lifts her hands to my face and closes her eyes. I feel everything I once thought I'd lost come home to me at once.

We don't rush the night. We move slowly, like the world is still watching, and we want to show it how love endures. Her dress slides from her shoulders. My hands shake, not from nerves but reverence. Her touch is steady. Familiar. Sacred. We don't say much. We don't need to. Because here, in the soft hush of our shared bed, beneath a roof we built together, with a garden outside blooming into tomorrow, there is nothing left to fear. Only this: That the years will pass too quickly. That the mornings will feel too brief. That every day with her will never be enough. But tonight, tonight we have time. Time to kiss slow. To whisper. To let the silence between us say what words can't. Long after the fire dims, I lie beside her and listen to her breathing. Outside, the garden rustles with wind and the memory of guests drifting home. Inside, the candle burns low, and Elena sleeps with one hand resting on my chest, her wedding ring glinting softly in the dark. And I think: If the world had ended years ago, I would never have known what it meant to be loved like this. To be seen. Chosen. Stayed with. To be hers. In the stillness.

I make a promise I've never spoken aloud: Tomorrow, I'll wake early. I'll make her coffee before the birds begin. I'll warm her slippers by the stove. I'll kiss the top of her head as she steps into the garden. And I'll spend every day after this one remembering that somehow — in the ruin of war, in the silence of exile, in the soft rise of spring, love found its way here. To us. To this small place beneath a blooming pear tree. Where she is mine. And I am hers. And we are finally, finally home. Morning comes slow. Not with urgency, not with alarms, but with soft golden light pushing its way through the curtains, and the gentle sound of birdsong nudging against the silence. I open my eyes to find her already awake beside me. Elena watches the ceiling, her hand still resting on my chest, her breathing light. "You slept," I whisper.

She turns her head toward me, a smile already tugging at her mouth. "So did you." We lie there for a while, unmoving. Wrapped in linen and peace and the scent of rosemary that still lingers in her hair. She reaches over to touch the edge of the window frame, where the light pools. "I dreamed of the pear tree," she says. "Oh?" "It was still blooming," she murmurs. "Even in winter." Later, we move through the house like we've lived here forever — which in some ways, we have. Not in years, but in intention. In every beam sanded smooth, in every pan hung neatly on its hook, in every sentence we've spoken in the soft hush between dusk and dawn. I make the coffee. She stands in the doorway, barefoot, her wedding ring catching the morning light. She doesn't speak. Just watches me with the kind of quiet that says: *this is what we were made for.* And I feel it — the full weight and grace of a beginning.

After breakfast, we walk out to the garden together. The soil is damp. The breeze is cool. The last of the wedding lanterns sway from the fence, still carrying the scent of wax and wildflowers. She kneels at the base of the tree, touching one of the fallen petals. "Everything's still here," she says. I nod. "And nothing is the same." She turns to look at me. "Do you think they'd believe it?" she asks softly. "The villagers back home. That we made it. That we got all the way here." I crouch beside her. "They believed in you more than you ever did." She smiles. Not in denial — in understanding. Because she believes it now too. We spend the day in the garden. No plan, no rush. We tend the soil. We prune the vines. We tie small signs to the seedlings so the children from the village can learn their names. And when the sun begins to set again, casting golden light over the cottage roof and the curved horizon, I look at her — hands in the dirt, her dark hair loose down, cheeks flushed with wind and work and something that looks like joy. And I think: **This is the rest of our life.** Not perfect. Not easy. But ours. Rooted in the earth, lit by the stars, and held together by the simple, sacred act of loving one another — day after day, season after season, from that first impossible moment in Sicily to this one: Here, in Hampshire.

Home.

Ana Monroy

The End.

Ana Monroy

Authors Note

A sweeping wartime love story of survival, sacrifice, and second chances.

Sicily, 1943. The world is collapsing, but Elena Santoro refuses to let hope die.
Living under the suffocating grip of German occupation, Elena shelters frightened children in a hidden cave while helping the villagers survive the daily cruelties of war. Her heart is worn but unbroken—until an Allied pilot crash-lands near her town, injured, hunted, and very much alive.
Flight Lieutenant Jack Branner never expected to fall for someone in the middle of a battlefield. But Elena is unlike anyone he's ever known courageous, clever, and determined to protect her people, even at the risk of her own life. Trapped together as the enemy closes in, Jack and Elena must forge a desperate plan to signal the Allies, outwit the Germans, and save the villagers hiding in the shadows.
As the bombs fall and the front lines shift, a fragile love begins to bloom between them—one born not of comfort, but of choice.
But when the war ends and peace returns, the hardest question remains:
Can love survive the silence after the storm?

From candlelit caves to a cottage in the English countryside, **Beneath a Sky of Hope** is a heart-stirring journey through loss, courage, and the transformative power of love. Perfect for readers of Kristin Hannah, Kate Quinn, and Jojo Moyes, this is a story that lingers long after the last page.

Beneath a Sky of Hope

Ana Monroy

Born in England, Ana Monroy discovered her passion for storytelling and embarked on her literary journey from a very young age. She has won several drama and literature competitions during her secondary school years in London. She has continued with her university studies, graduating as an Aviation Engineer with Honours and completing her Postgraduate studies in the Aerospace discipline at Kingston University. She has found encouragement and inspiration to dedicate herself to writing fiction with heart and purpose, specializing in contemporary romance, finding strong and complex women as protagonists. Her first novel explores themes such as love, healing, and the search for a home in unexpected places, she combines emotional depth with everyday magic. Her stories resonate with readers who believe it's never too late to rewrite their own narrative. She hopes to continue to create moving, character-driven novels that speak to men and women at every stage of their lives.

This book is available in both forms, as an E-Kindle and paperback format

Beneath a Sky of Hope

Ana Monroy

Beneath a Sky of Hope

Printed in Dunstable, United Kingdom